"You'd be my wife right now if—"

Adam began coldly, then couldn't finish. He could only shake his head and search Kirsten's eyes.

"It doesn't matter anymore, Adam," Kirsten said softly.

"The hell it doesn't. What did that bastard you married have on you that was so bad it made you miss our wedding day? Made you leave the man you *claimed* to love standing alone in a country church with half the town looking on? Made you—"

"Adam, please, don't…" Kirsten interrupted, then lowered her head and closed her eyes, the tears stinging.

He gripped her arms. "I want to know what made you marry a man you didn't love," he finished. "I want to know why, Kirsten."

Kirsten looked up at him and let him see into her eyes, see the love burning there. The secrets. And the fear that those secrets would be found out…

Dear Reader,

Once again, we've rounded up the best romantic reading for you right here in Silhouette Intimate Moments. Start off with Maggie Shayne's *The Baddest Bride in Texas,* part of her top-selling miniseries THE TEXAS BRAND, and you'll see what I mean. Secrets, steam and romance…this book has everything.

And how many of you have been following that baby? A lot, I'll bet. And this month our FOLLOW THAT BABY cross-line miniseries concludes with *The Mercenary and the New Mom,* by Merline Lovelace. At last the baby's found—and there's romance in the air, as well.

If Western loving's your thing, we've got a trio of books to keep you happy. *Home Is Where the Cowboy Is,* by Doreen Roberts, launches a terrific new miniseries called RODEO MEN. THE SULLIVAN BROTHERS continue their wickedly sexy ways in *Heartbreak Ranch,* by Kylie Brant. And Cheryl Biggs's *The Cowboy She Never Forgot*—a book *you'll* find totally memorable—sports our WAY OUT WEST flash. Then complete your month's reading with *Suddenly a Family,* by Leann Harris. This FAMILIES ARE FOREVER title features an adorable set of twins, their delicious dad and the woman who captures all three of their hearts.

Enjoy them all—then come back next month for six more wonderful Intimate Moments novels, the most exciting romantic reading around.

Yours,

Leslie J. Wainger
Executive Senior Editor

Please address questions and book requests to:
Silhouette Reader Service
U.S.: 3010 Walden Ave., P.O. Box 1325, Buffalo, NY 14269
Canadian: P.O. Box 609, Fort Erie, Ont. L2A 5X3

Maggie Shayne

THE BADDEST BRIDE IN TEXAS

Silhouette®

INTIMATE™ MOMENTS®

Published by Silhouette Books

America's Publisher of Contemporary Romance

SILHOUETTE BOOKS

ISBN 0-373-07907-9

THE BADDEST BRIDE IN TEXAS

Copyright © 1999 by Margaret Benson

Printed in U.S.A.

MAGGIE SHAYNE,

a national bestselling author whom *Romantic Times Magazine* calls "brilliantly inventive," has written more than fifteen novels for Silhouette. Her Silhouette single-title release *Born in Twilight* (3/97) was based on her popular vampire series for Shadows, WINGS IN THE NIGHT.

Maggie has won numerous awards, including a *Romantic Times Magazine* Career Achievement Award. A three-time finalist for the Romance Writers of America's prestigious RITA Award, Maggie also writes mainstream contemporary fantasy.

In her spare time Maggie enjoys collecting gemstones, reading tarot cards, hanging out on the Genie computer network and spending time outdoors. She lives in a rural town in central New York with her husband, Rick, five beautiful daughters and a bulldog named Wrinkles.

Chapter 1

"So, what do you think, big brother?" Adam Brand sat at his brother's desk with the chair tipped back and his feet propped up. He tapped his fingers in time with Hank Jr. on the radio. Other than that, he didn't move much at all. Garrett was too busy to complain.

"What do I think?" Garrett glanced up from where he stood, elbow-deep in the ancient file cabinet on the other side of his office. "I think you volunteered to help me out today, and so far all you've done is sit there bouncing career plans off me."

Okay, so Garrett *wasn't* too busy to complain. Adam grinned and slapped his boots onto the floor, sitting up straight and leaning over the keyboard again. "I've *been* helping. Just bouncing ideas off you as I go along." He finished entering the information from the file folder in front of him to the new computer on

Garrett's desk. Then he closed the folder and added it to the "done" pile. "So what do you think?"

Garrett shrugged, carrying a fresh stack of files to the desk and dropping them down. The front door was open, but the only breeze right now came from the little electric fan in the corner, not from the dusty west Texas air.

"I never saw the appeal of number crunching, myself, Adam. You seem to do well enough with it, though." Garrett parted his lips, then closed them again. He didn't say any more.

"Why do I sense a 'but' dying to jump in here?"

Garrett met Adam's eyes and shrugged, making the shiny silver badge on his shirt move up and down. "I don't know, Adam. Guess I kinda figured you'd get bored with it after a while. You went to the big city to lick your wounds, and that was understandable. But being a banker for the rest of your life? Hell, I never thought I'd see one of us…" He bit his lip, probably sensing he was treading close to dangerous ground.

Adam sat up straighter and tried to hold on to his temper. It wasn't hard. He'd been practicing for a long time. "Lick my wounds, huh? Is that what everybody thinks?"

Garrett lowered his head. "Nobody blames you. Kirsten stood you up at the altar, Adam. Took off and married another man. No one expected you to get over it all at once."

"I'm over it. I've *been* over it."

"Okay." Garrett nodded and turned away. "You say you're over it, you're over it."

Adam got to his feet. "I *am!*"

"Hey, whatever you say. I don't want to fight with you," Garrett said, holding up both hands.

It would have been funny if Adam hadn't been so disgusted at his brother's mistaken assumptions. Garrett stood a head taller and outweighed him by fifty pounds. Not that Adam was a small man. Just that his brother was a bear.

"You'll never understand," Adam said.

"Probably not."

And Adam knew he was right. Hell, it ought to be obvious how different he was from his brother—from his entire family—just at a glance. Garrett's jeans were faded blue, worn white in places. His boots were scuffed. His shirt found at the local discount store for $9.99.

Adam's boots gleamed, and he wore jeans only to do chores. The rest of the time he dressed the way he always had: well. Today he wore black trousers with a matching Armani shirt, band collar. They all drove pickups or SUVs. He drove a Jaguar. They all picked on him for his so-called big-city ways. Except for Garrett's wife, Chelsea, who claimed he was trying to compensate for a broken heart and the resulting feelings of inadequacy by buying nice things for himself. He didn't know why the hell Garrett had ever encouraged that woman to go for her degree in psychology. Adam felt defensive; about his life-style, his clothes, his car and his plans for the future. And he wondered briefly why.

"I think I could do well here," he said slowly. "Set

up an office, keep the books for some local businesses, offer investment counseling…''

''I'm sure you could. And hell, I'm all for anything that keeps you home.'' Garrett sent him a warm smile. ''It's where you belong, Adam.''

Adam nodded. ''At least we agree on one thing. I've missed it. New York's great, but it sure as hell isn't Texas.''

''Sure as hell isn't,'' Garrett agreed. He cleared his throat, licked his lips.

''What is it you're deciding not to say?'' Adam asked.

Garrett looked sheepish. ''I just don't see why the original plan couldn't do just as well.'' He talked slow, taking his time. Garrett always talked slow, measured every word.

''Original plan?'' Adam frowned.

''You, uh…used to talk about a dude ranch. Don't you remember?''

''Oh, that.'' He tried to sound as if he'd forgotten all about it. That had been *their* dream. His and Kirsten's. He didn't let himself think about that anymore. ''Hell, Garrett, that must've been a hundred years ago.'' It wasn't. It wasn't so long ago at all. But a lot had happened since then. His dreams had been thrown back in his face one too many times, and Adam had decided dreaming was a foolish thing to do. Practicality was better. Safer.

''Shoot,'' Garrett muttered as he opened another file. ''The rest of this one's in the back room. Along with a few others I'd forgotten about. I'll get 'em.''

He slapped another file on the desk and headed out of the office.

Poor Garrett. He'd thought the new computer system the town had purchased for the sheriff's department would be a blessing. A work saver. Instead, it was turning into the world's biggest headache. Fine time for his deputy-slash-brother-in-law to be out of town. Still, it made Adam smile to think of his baby sister Jessi doing Walt Disney World with her husband and little girl. He hoped they'd bring back plenty of pictures.

The phone rang, and Adam automatically snatched it up. "Sheriff's office."

Silence.

"Hello? Can I—"

"Adam?"

Her voice was so soft he barely recognized it at first. But it wasn't as if he could forget the sound of his name on Kirsten's lips, even when she only breathed it, the way she'd done just now.

Especially when she only breathed it the way she'd done just now.

A heavy, hot fist plowed right into his belly. For a second he couldn't draw air. Then he managed to inhale, and uttered a single word.

"Kirsten," he said. Great. A croak. His throat was drier than a tumbleweed. He reminded himself that he *hated* this woman. Hated her in a way he'd never hated anyone before. And he *liked* hating her. It felt good to hate her. He *needed* to hate her. "What do *you* want?" There, that was better. Much better.

She was silent for a long moment. Then, "I...need to speak to Garrett."

"He's busy."

"It's not a social call, Adam. Please put your brother on the phone."

Adam blinked, because there was something in her voice. Something that hadn't been there in all the times he'd spoken to her since he'd been back here. All those times, there had been only ice. Cold and smooth and gleamingly perfect, without so much as a single chip in its frigid surface.

There was a chip now. And he cursed himself for wondering why.

"I'm helping Garrett out today," he said slowly, telling himself that his curiosity was natural and meant nothing at all. "Tell me what you want, and I'll pass it along."

"Fine," she whispered. "Fine. You want to know so bad, Adam, I'll tell you. My husband is lying here on the floor with a small bullet hole in the middle of his forehead. If Garrett's not too busy, maybe he'd like to come on out here and—"

Adam swore, and she stopped talking. She couldn't be serious. But she was; it was clear in her voice. He'd always known her better than anyone. That hadn't changed. He cupped the receiver. "Garrett, get in here." Then he spoke to Kirsten again. "You okay?"

"I'm standing here with his blood on my hands, Adam. How the hell am I supposed to answer that?"

"Is anyone else in the house?"

A brief pause. A shaky sigh that seemed to catch in

her throat. "I...don't think so. Tell Garrett to hurry, Adam. He could come back...."

Garrett came in from the back room, glanced once at Adam and instantly frowned. Adam looked back, but his words were for Kirsten, the woman he hated. And there was a big lump of fear in his throat; fear that maybe she was none too safe right now, and that maybe by the time he could get out there, she would be lying on the floor beside the bastard she'd married.

"We'll be there in two minutes, Kirsten. Stay where you are, and don't touch anything, okay?"

She might have nodded. He never knew. The connection died with a click that was way too final and unannounced for Adam's peace of mind.

She'd heard an odd sound. Just once. A muted "pop." Nothing more. She'd been lying outside by the pool, soaking up the sun in her designer suit, wearing her Ray Bans. But the odd sound had sent such a strange, creepy feeling up her spine that she'd been unable to ignore it. And the silence that followed seemed heavy. It had been quiet before. But this was different. The birds had gone still. Even the bugs had stopped buzzing. And the hum of the pool's all but silent filter pump seemed suddenly ominous.

She got up, pulled on her white terry wrap and padded barefoot through the glass doors and into the sprawling, cold house. But it was empty. Her voice only echoed from the walls as she called out, and a coldness shivered up her spine.

She moved through the house, bare feet curling re-

flexively against the cold Italian marble after the
warmth of the sunbaked tiles around the pool. She saw
no one and finally ventured into the study when she
saw the light on in there.

She rarely went into Joseph's study. She rarely went
anywhere she was likely to run into him. She detested
the man. It was no secret—between the two of them,
at least. He knew it, and hated her in return. He'd
ruined her life, forced her into a loveless marriage,
made her miserable. In return, she focused her energy
on making him just as miserable. Eventually he would
have all he could stand of her. He would let her go.
Until then, she would play the role he'd designed for
her. She would be the rich bitch who had dumped a
fine man and run off with an old geezer just to get her
hands on his fortune. She would let the entire town go
on hating her guts. And she would keep her emotions
turned off for good.

"Joseph?" she called, stepping into the study. The
smells here were familiar…and yet there was something different. Musty old books and hardwood, cigar
smoke lingering in the air. But what was that pun-
gence? Sulphur and heat…and something else…

Then she saw him, and her feet froze in place as
she felt her body heat drain away, leaving her cold
and immobile. He lay on his back on the floor. He
wore forest green silk pajamas and a matching robe,
the sash still tied around his ample middle. His favorite velour slippers, one half off his foot. A large pool
of blood was spreading slowly over the floor beneath
the back of his head. A neat dark hole the size of her

little finger stood like a Hindu's jewel in the center of his forehead.

A jolt like an electric shock went through her. Her spine went so rigid she thought it might snap, and a scream leapt to her lips, but she bit it back. Swallowing the fear, the shock, she forced herself to move closer. With one foot she nudged his head, turning it slightly to see where all the blood was coming from, then turning away in disgust. There wasn't a hell of a lot left of the back of her husband's skull. She shouldn't have looked. She *really* shouldn't have looked.

Nausea rose. She pushed it down. Tremors set in. She fought them into submission. Dead? Was the bastard *truly* dead?

"Joseph?" She forced herself to look at him again, to look closely.

No answer. She nudged him again with her toe, grimacing as she realized she was standing barefoot in the spreading crimson puddle. Nothing. Finally, she bent down and pressed her fingers to his limp wrist in search of a pulse. But there was none. And he wasn't breathing.

A small black revolver lay on the floor beside him. The blood pool spread slowly to embrace it.

Kirsten felt no emotion. She hadn't let herself feel any powerful emotions since the day she'd married this dead man on the floor. That day had been the beginning of a prison sentence for her. And if she could have felt anything at all right now, it would have been relief. But she'd grown too wary, too cautious, too controlled, to allow herself to feel even that.

She turned to the desk, picked up the phone and placed her call to the sheriff's office. Garrett Brand might still dislike her for what she'd done to his brother two years ago, but he was an honest man who took his job very seriously. And he wasn't far away.

A small tremor of fear shivered up her spine when the idea first occurred to her that Joseph wouldn't have done this to himself. That someone else must have done it. That they might still be around. But she stamped the fear out. She was above fear. She didn't feel anything she didn't *want* to feel.

Then Adam's voice came across the line instead of Garrett's. Adam. Again something rocked her composure. Again she fought it and won.

Unlike his brother, Adam didn't dislike her. He actively hated her. And she didn't blame him. It occurred to her that maybe now she would finally be free to tell him the truth. To clear her conscience once and for all. He would hate her all the more, but that didn't really matter. He had a right to know. She had a right to unburden herself. The secret had been kept for far too long. She'd destroyed Adam Brand's life in more ways than he even realized.

But first things first. She told him Joseph had been murdered. Then she hung up the phone.

There was a sound behind her.

She went motionless as her back felt suddenly naked and under scrutiny. Calm. She had to be calm. It could be Phillip, Joseph's driver and all-around right-hand man. It could be Sally, the housekeeper. It could be anyone.

It could be the killer.

She turned slowly, saw the masked figure standing in the open doorway, fought the panic that made her entire body begin to tremble. He was dressed in black and seemed like some dark phantom, and for the first time she realized that her life was in danger.

He took a step toward her, one hand reaching out, mouth opening as if he were about to say something. Without missing a beat, she dropped to her knees in the red slickness and clawed the slippery gun into her hands. She lifted it. "Don't come any closer." Her hands were shaking so hard that she would never hit him if she fired a hundred times. But he wouldn't know that.

He kept coming, faster than before. Squeezing her eyes tight, Kirsten pulled the trigger. The weapon exploded in her hands, bucking backward with the recoil. When she opened her eyes, the killer was gone.

A siren wailed outside, grew louder, then stopped. She stood where she was, gripping the gun, watching the door, chanting a mental mantra. *Control. Control. Control.*

Adam came in first. He stood in the open double doors, looking as if he'd just stepped off the cover of some special Texas issue of *GQ*. While she stood in a white bikini and matching terry wrap and a whole lot of blood, with a murder weapon in one hand. She always did know how to accessorize, she thought a little crazily.

Adam just stood there, looking from Kirsten to Joseph's body, to the gun in her hand. She read his face. She'd always been good at reading his face. His beautiful face. And that was when she realized what she'd done.

He held up a hand. "Put the gun down, Kirsten."

She looked at it. Cold and black and evil, wobbling heavily in her bloody hand. She lowered the barrel slowly, then let the weapon fall to the floor. Adam came forward then. He gripped her shoulders, looking her over with an urgency she didn't understand. Until she glanced down and saw all the blood. Smears and streaks of a dead man's blood on her hands, her arms, her bare feet, her legs. It painted bright patterns on her Versace bikini and once-immaculate white wrap.

"Where are you hurt? Where are you hurt?" he kept asking.

"It's not me," she managed. "It's Joseph's blood. He's dead." Control. She had to get control. She was going to be a quivering mess soon if she didn't get hold of herself.

Garrett was in the house. She saw him pass by the doors in his big hat, weapon drawn, apparently going from room to room. Searching for the killer, she guessed. He wouldn't find him.

"I told you not to touch anything," Adam was saying. Holding her arm, he drew her around the big desk she'd always hated, and the blood made her feet sticky against the floor tiles. Adam pressed her into a creaking chair that held the scent of Joseph's illegal Cuban cigars. "Damn, Kirsten, why did you pick up the gun?"

Adam didn't smell like cigars. He smelled like fresh Texas sunshine and new leather. The band of the Stetson he wore, maybe, or his belt, or maybe his boots. She liked a man who smelled like leather. Texas men, real ones, usually did. She lifted her head, met his eyes. Those eyes. She'd seen so much in them once. But that was over. More over than he could even guess. And there was nothing in his eyes for her now except speculation and questions.

"The killer came back," she said, and she thought her voice sounded calm. In control. "He...came at me, and I just...reacted."

Adam's face remained expressionless. "Did you fire at him?"

She nodded. Adam swore.

Garrett came in then, pausing to shake his head at the sight of Joseph, then reaching to check for a pulse just as Kirsten had done.

"He's dead," she told him unnecessarily.

Garrett looked at her, worry in his eyes. "There's no sign of anyone else in the house. Are you all right, Kirsten?"

She nodded. Then jerked a little as more sirens sounded outside. Cars skidded, and men came charging into the house. Several of them flooded the study, and Kirsten tugged her wrap more tightly around her and sat still, not cringing, not cowering, and forcibly not clinging to Adam Brand. She hadn't expected Garrett to notify the Texas Rangers right away. She'd thought he would handle this himself.

"Kirsten Cowan?" one of them asked.

She nodded. Garrett stepped up. "I'm the sheriff here, Ranger. I wasn't aware you'd been called."

"Well, we were. So as long as we're here—"

"It's my town, Ranger."

"It's a capital crime, Sheriff."

Garrett didn't back down. "Looks like a suicide to me. But time will tell. Who called you?"

The ranger shrugged. "Call came from this number. Caller hung up without giving a name."

Kirsten's blood went cold. "I didn't call you," she muttered. "And no one else was here...except the killer."

Garrett looked at her. The rangers looked at her. She would have clarified the statement, but she had a feeling her voice would come out weak and shaky if she tried.

Then Adam came to the rescue. "It was no suicide," he said. "Kirsten saw the killer."

One of the rangers came forward with a plastic bag and picked up the gun, dropping it in. Kirsten was all too aware that her fingerprints were all over it. Closing her eyes, she called the killer's image to mind. Had he been wearing gloves? Black gloves that matched the rest of his clothes? She thought so.

"We're going to want you to come back to the El Paso station with us, Mrs. Cowan. Answer some questions."

"Garrett..." Adam began.

Garrett met his brother's eyes and nodded. "Ranger, Ms. Cowan is in no state to be answering questions right now. What do you say we let her get changed, give her some time—"

The ranger eyed Kirsten. "No showers. And we'll want the clothes you're wearing." He glanced at Garrett. "If you can assure me you'll see to that, then I have no objections."

Garrett nodded. "You could question her right here in town. My office is just—"

"I want her at the station."

"Okay," Garrett said. "Okay. I'll bring her in myself."

The ranger nodded, then sent a pointed glance at Adam. "Who're you?"

Kirsten could almost hear the man's assumptions. That Adam was the "other man." That this was all the result of some sordid love triangle. It would have been funny if the situation hadn't been so dire. She almost laughed, and brought her hands to her mouth to prevent it...then the would-be laugh became a gag when she glimpsed the drying blood that coated her hands as they hovered in midair near her face.

Her knees gave, just a little, before she snapped them rigid again. Adam's arm went around her waist.

"Get her out of here, Adam. I'll field the rangers' questions," Garrett said.

Adam nodded, kept his arm where it was and guided her out of the room.

His hand on her was gentle but firm. Supportive. As

if he thought she might need his strength to keep her upright and mobile.

She didn't.

She took a step away to let him know that. And instantly felt weakness set in. Her pace slowed. Her knees quivered. His hand returned, but to her arm this time. A less intimate embrace, but every bit as strong and supportive.

"Hold on," he muttered.

He guided her to the stairs and up them. He didn't let go again. She didn't ask him to. She didn't *want* him to. And she hated her own lack of strength and resolve.

"Where's your bedroom?"

She licked paper-dry lips, but the effect was minimal. "This way." Like a bullfrog's croak, her voice. She turned down the hallway, but paused to look at the stains her feet were making in the carpet. Glancing backward down the stairs, she saw that she'd left a trail of them, each one a little darker, all the way to the bottom.

"It'll clean," Adam said.

"I don't care. I really don't. In fact, I hope it's ruined. I hope they have to tear it up. Hell, I hope they burn this place to the ground."

He looked at her, eyes soft and blue and puzzled. "That's an odd thing to say."

"Is it?"

He searched her face. "What the hell happened here this morning, Kirsten?"

She shrugged. "The king is dead," she whispered,

not even sure why. But slowly, slowly, a weight seemed to be lifting from her shoulders. The yoke of slavery. Of bondage. Of imprisonment. That was what her two years with Joseph Cowan had been. Was she free of him now? Was it even possible?

"Long live the freaking queen." She muttered the phrase in a whisper and turned toward her room. And she mashed her bloody footprints into the carpet as she walked.

Chapter 2

She didn't say another word, but then again, maybe she didn't need to. She'd said too much already, and Adam found himself absurdly glad he was the only one who'd heard the sarcasm in her voice. She hardly seemed to fit the role of the grieving widow just now. And what the hell was he supposed to make of that?

She walked with purpose along the palatial corridor with the thick carpet that had, by now, wiped her feet clean. Finally she paused just outside the huge hardwood bedroom door. An ornate bench sat against the wall alongside it. Cherry, he thought. Probably an antique. Straight backed, thin cushioned and claw footed, it looked about as comfortable for sitting as a half-starved, swaybacked nag, but he guessed that was what she wanted him to do. She caught his eye, nodded at the bench, then ducked her hoity-toity hiney right through the bedroom door without missing a beat. And she closed it behind her. Not hard, but not gently. Just firmly enough to send the message.

Stay out.

Sure. Okay, he could handle that.

Adam sat. He could hear the distant, muffled voices of the men downstairs, and the vehicles coming and going outside. The place was going to be a circus for the rest of the day. Forensics teams would be in and out. He'd thought Cowan's death was pretty obviously a suicide...until Kirsten said she'd fired at a masked intruder.

Adam's throat went dry. For a second down there he'd thought he'd seen the old Kirsten peering out from behind her ice-coated eyes. The real Kirsten. The girl she used to be back when she'd loved him more than she'd loved an old man's money.

Or maybe that Kirsten *hadn't* been real after all. Maybe this was the real Kirsten, complete with ice water running in her veins and a face so glasslike and emotionless it would crack if she smiled.

The bench was every bit as inhospitable as it looked. When his back started aching in protest, he got up and paced. Studied the framed print of a fairy trying to enchant some poor fool of a knight. ''Big mistake, pal,'' Adam warned, but from the stunned expression on the knight's face, it looked as if he was already too late. ''Big mistake.'' There was no sound from beyond the bedroom door. And the longer Kirsten took, the more antsy Adam got. A half hour ticked by. He was halfway to thinking maybe she'd climbed out a window and was even now headed for the border. It had gone quiet downstairs. Sounded as if the rangers had packed up and gone, for the moment. But their forensics crews would be back soon enough. Still, if she *had* slipped out, maybe no one would have seen....

But that was stupid. She wouldn't run. She had no reason to. Not unless...

The photo clicked into place in his head, that scene he'd walked in on a short while ago appearing in freeze-frame in his mind. Kirsten standing over her husband's dead body, blood on her clothes, a gun clutched in her hand. In her eyes a killing frost, and maybe...just maybe...a hint of relief.

But she couldn't have done it.

Wrong, a little voice inside him muttered. The old Kirsten couldn't have done it. Kirsten Armstrong. The girl with the barely suppressed wild side and the zest for living that got her into trouble more often than not. The girl who'd loved him.

That wasn't who she was anymore.

Adam hadn't seen her often in the years since she'd run off with old man Cowan. Not often. But often enough to know she was a different woman now. And the change was so thorough, it was as if the old Kirsten had been put to rest—dead and buried.

Now she dressed like a woman out to impress, and she wore her clothes like armor. Cold, carefully chosen conservative designer suits in harsh primary colors. And everything matching, all the time. The skirts matched the blouses matched the jackets matched the nylons, shoes, bag.... She was too put together now. As if maybe she were hiding something. Hair, always perfect. Makeup, always complete. Nails, always polished to a glossy shine.

She never smiled anymore.

This Kirsten was not the woman he'd known. Maybe this Kirsten was entirely capable of murder. No way to tell for sure.

Adam got more uneasy as those thoughts assailed him. He heaved a sigh, expelling the last of his patience along with his breath, marched to the door and rapped three times.

No answer.

He tried the knob.

It turned, and he stepped hesitantly inside.

His first thought was that this was more like an apartment than a bedroom. It was a freaking suite. Complete with all the amenities.

Kirsten sat at a dressing table with a tube of lipstick in one hand. She met his gaze in the mirror. "Are they gone yet?"

Her hair was dry now and freshly styled. Sprayed to within an inch of its life, he thought. Her eyes were lined and shadowed, and every trace of shock or trauma her face might reveal was buried under makeup. She wore Armani. White. Spotless, sterile white. Leg-hugging skintight pants with little slits at the ankles, and strappy white sandals on her feet. White sleeveless blouse, tucked in. Nice and neat. White bolero jacket on the back of her chair, ready to don. White opals in her ears, pearls at her throat. Even the damned wristband on her damned diamond-studded Bulova was white.

Adam tore his gaze away from her and took a quick glance around the room, saw the open door to the adjoining bathroom, the wet footprints, the damp towels, the steamed-up mirrors. "You showered?" he asked her in disbelief. "Kirsten, they told you—"

"I don't give a damn what they told me." Her words were measured, level. She capped the lipstick tube, set it down with a precise click. It tipped over. She reached to right it and knocked it off the stand. Then she went still and clasped her hands around each other to hide the fact that they were so unsteady she could barely hold them still. Her face was a mask, both literally and figuratively. But her tension showed in those pale, shaking hands.

"I had Joseph's blood all over me, Adam. They couldn't expect me to just leave it." She returned her gaze to her own reflection, met her own eyes and looked away so fast it made Adam wonder why. "So are they gone?"

"Yeah," Adam said, staring at her back and wondering what the hell had happened to the Kirsten he'd known. "For now. They'll be back."

"Why am I not surprised?"

He stepped farther into the room. There were a lot of things unsaid between the two of them. He supposed it ought to seem strange to be here and not say them. Not ask her why…and yet it was for the best. It didn't matter why. He was over her. And this was neither the time nor the place for questions about their past. For quite a while he'd been going along as if it had never happened, and he thought he'd pretty well got the hang of it by now. A little game of make-believe. Making believe he'd never felt a thing for her. Forgetting every night he'd spent with her body wrapped around him. Pretending none of it had ever happened.

He met her eyes in the mirror. For just an instant he thought he saw those same memories flash and vanish. As if she were pretending, too.

"Do you have any idea who did this, Kirsten?"

She turned around to face him this time. "Why don't you say what you mean, Adam? You're asking if *I* did it, aren't you?"

"No, he's not."

Kirsten looked up fast. Adam turned to see his brother in the doorway. Garrett stepped inside, noted the evidence of her recent shower, thinned his lips, but didn't comment. "But those rangers are gonna be asking you just that, and soon. They'll find your prints on that weapon. And if you fired it, powder burn traces on your hands. Traces that are going to show up whether you showered or not."

"They don't need to check for that," she told Garrett. "I freely admit I fired the gun. Once. At the killer. What was I supposed to do, let him murder me, too?"

"You say once. They'll say twice. Once at a make-believe intruder, to validate your alibi, and once at your husband. Now, maybe if they find another set of prints on that gun—a set that doesn't belong to you or to Joseph—then they'll believe your story."

Kirsten bit her lip, averting her eyes abruptly. Adam found his gaze focused on her hands again. Her expressionless face told him nothing. It was all in the hands. They clenched into fists in her lap, perfectly painted nails digging into her palms.

"I think the killer was wearing gloves, Garrett."

"Great," Adam said, rolling his eyes and expelling all the air in his lungs at once. "That's just great."

"You say that as if it's my fault. I didn't dress the man, Adam."

Adam looked at her. God, she sounded so cold. So unmoved. Didn't she even care that the guy she'd been married to for two years had just been zipped into a body bag?

"All they'll be lacking is motive, Kirsten," Garrett said slowly. "I think you probably ought to contact a lawyer."

She closed her eyes, opened them again. "I didn't kill him." She folded her hands together as if to hold them still.

"Hell, Kirsten, I know that." Garrett sounded sincere, and that surprised Adam. How could his brother be so sure of her when even *he* had his doubts? "You'd still best get yourself a lawyer," Garrett went on. "Once they confirm that Joseph left everything to you in his will, it's gonna be—"

Kirsten exhaled in a burst, a sarcastic kind of sound. "He didn't leave me a nickel, Garrett. He'd rather burn in hell than see me with his precious money. Trust me, I won't be named in my husband's will."

Garrett frowned and sent Adam a questioning look.

Adam shrugged and tried not to let his shock show on his face. He didn't like the way her declaration had made his stomach clench up tight. The way his brain had whispered what his foolish heart hadn't wanted to believe two years ago. That Kirsten would never marry for money. That if she married old Joseph Cowan it had to be because she loved him.

Maybe that love had gone bad, but if the cash hadn't been her motive…then what else was there?

And why the hell did it feel as if she'd just stabbed him in the back all over again, only with a blade made of ice this time, instead of the red-hot steel she'd skewered him with before?

"Why wouldn't your husband name you as his heir?" Garrett was asking. "You were his wife. He had no children."

"Not for lack of trying," she said, a slight curl marring the perfection of her tinted upper lip for just an instant. A brief lapse. Then she wore the glass face again. The one that told Adam nothing. He glanced down. Her fingers were claws now, nails gripping her thighs like talons gripping meat. She was holding on as if for dear life.

Tough to care when her words hit Adam like a two-by-four in the softest part of his belly. One more blow to the midsection and he would be reeling.

She's been married to the man for over two years. Did I really think they never had sex? That the old geezer never laid his cold, arthritic hands on her?

Kirsten pressed her lips tight, as if to keep herself

from saying any more. Her gaze slid to Adam's; then she turned away.

"It doesn't matter why. I won't inherit a thing, and therefore..." her head came up slowly. "Therefore...I had no motive. They aren't going to arrest me without a motive, are they, Garrett?"

Garrett didn't answer. "You ready to go to El Paso now? They want you to make a statement, maybe answer a few questions."

She looked scared for just a second. A slight widening in those eyes that had, until now, been like sheets of brown ice. Her hands unfolded, trembled visibly against the leggings, their skin nearly as pale as the white they lay upon. But a second later she pressed her palms together and stilled her features. "I suppose now is as good a time as any."

She wanted to know why Adam was coming along to El Paso. But she didn't ask. Kirsten didn't see Lash Monroe anywhere, so she assumed the deputy was unavailable and Adam was filling in. But in that case, Adam should be back at the office, manning the phones and holding down the fort, shouldn't he?

Right. As if any calls were likely to come in. In a town as small as Quinn, a sheriff could work once a week and keep up with the load. Most of the time.

No one spoke in the giant-sized pickup. Garrett drove, his ten-gallon hat shading his eyes from the brilliant sun. She'd been relegated to the center spot, and Adam was wedged in beside her, his smaller, sexier Stetson hat shadowing his face so she couldn't see his eyes. Couldn't tell what he might be thinking or feeling. He was touching her. Not liking it, she imagined, but touching her. His thigh pressed up against hers, and she could feel the warmth seeping from the flesh under his black trousers to the flesh under her white leggings.

She'd missed that kind of warmth for a long time. Then she'd stopped missing it. It was something she'd learned to do without. Which, she supposed, would come in real handy should she wind up spending the rest of her life in some prison cell.

That wouldn't happen, though. She would be okay. Garrett had called Joseph's lawyer, Stephen Hawkins, and the old man had agreed to meet them at the El Paso rangers' station. Nobody was going to arrest her, she thought. Not yet, anyway. Because once they saw the will, they would realize she had no motive.

None that they would know of. Kirsten *did* have motive, though. Her husband had blackmailed her into marrying him, had held her deepest secret, her most private nightmare, over her head for all this time. She'd been more prisoner than wife. And she'd wished Joseph Cowan dead a thousand times. But they wouldn't know that.

Not if she didn't tell.

She glanced at Adam and swallowed her regret. He'd lived without knowing the truth for this long. Maybe he didn't *need* to know. Maybe no one would *ever* need to know. It was a huge relief to realize that the one person who could expose her for what she'd done long ago was dead. And no one else knew. No one else ever would.

Adam's thigh moved slightly against hers. Heat and friction. Desire slammed her in the belly so hard she lost her breath.

No! Not now. Not anymore. That part of her was dead and buried. Especially where Adam was concerned.

She peered up at him. He was looking back at her. Her lips were dry, her face hot.

''It's gonna be okay,'' he said, and damned if he didn't sound like the same sweet cowboy she'd been in love with a hundred years ago, instead of the bitter, urban businessman he'd become.

''I know it is.'' Stupid reply. She should have said, ''I thought you hated my guts. Best keep right on hating them, Adam.'' But no. No Brand alive would treat a woman badly when she was facing this kind of trouble. Not even when that woman was her.

Hawkins was at the station when they arrived, gray suit impeccable, white hair unruly. He had a quiet dignity about him that Kirsten had always liked. A dignity that shone through even here, in a dingy, cluttered office with papers and files and empty throwaway cups strewn over every available inch of space. Wastebaskets overflowed; a watercooler gurgled; coffee rings marred manila folders and typed sheets. Uniformed men and women bumped and brushed one another as they hurried back and forth. In the midst of it all, Hawkins stood. Like a throwback to Mark Twain. A sweet Southern gentleman, an aging cavalier. He sent her a gentle smile that was condolence, affection and encouragement all at once, even before he made his way amid crisscrossing bodies toward her. She trusted him, even though he had been Joseph's attorney since the dawn of time, as far as she knew. She trusted him because he'd been her father's friend, even before all of that. And he still visited her dad in that Dallas nursing home every chance he got. That made him trustworthy in her book. Anyone who loved her father...

"Hello, Kirsten," he said, clasping her hands in his powder-soft, wrinkled ones. "Are you all right?" His pale blue eyes were dull. He smelled of camphor.

"I've been better, Stephen."

He looked past her, nodded to Garrett, then looked puzzled as he recognized Adam.

"Right in here, folks," a ranger called, and he held open a door. Beyond it she could see a dim room, a bare table, a couple of hard-looking chairs.

She swallowed hard, took a step forward. Adam moved up beside her and fell into step. And for a second it felt incredibly reassuring to let herself think he would be in that little interrogation room with her. Then she asked herself what the hell she was doing.

A cop slapped a hand on Adam's shoulder. "Just the lady and her lawyer, *amigo.*"

Adam stopped, and for just an instant he met her eyes. He drew his gaze away so quickly she almost couldn't read what was going on in his mind. And then it clicked into place, and she blinked in surprise. It was a question she'd glimpsed in his eyes just now. My God, he wanted to know if he should insist on coming in there with her. Fight his way in, if need be. And she knew he would, if she so much as nodded an affirmation. He'd get in, too. There were two Brand men in this station, not one alone. Garrett would back his brother up, right or wrong, the way one Brand always backed another one up no matter what. And against two determined Brands, this station full of Texas Rangers wouldn't stand a chance.

She had no right to ask for their help or their support. Not after what she'd done to them. And letting herself get dependent on any Brand now—*especially* Adam—would be a huge mistake.

She spoke to Adam, drawing his gaze back to hers again. ''I've been looking out for myself for a long time now, Adam. I'll be fine.'' He didn't look convinced. She could have kicked herself for leaning on him, even a little bit. Hell, if she started looking like a lady in distress, he would get the idea it was time to mount up and come to the rescue. She knew him too well. ''Besides,'' she added in as cool a tone as she could manage, ''this really isn't your problem.''

''Or my business, right?'' he asked, interpreting her words just the way she'd wanted him to.

''You said it. I didn't.''

Stephen Hawkins took her elbow in a gentle grip and escorted her into the room. She sat down at the empty table and glanced toward the door just before it closed. Adam stood there looking at her, his brows bent. But the frown wasn't angry. It was puzzled, curious...*searching*. And that was not good.

* * *

Adam paced. Garrett caught him on one of his repetitive trips back and forth across the width of the station's makeshift waiting room—a cubicle with three plastic chairs and a coffeepot—and stopped him by stepping into his path.

"So, this is…what? Your impression of a fellow being completely over the woman who jilted him? The one he claims he doesn't even like?"

Adam went still, looked up at his brother. "Being over her doesn't mean I want to see her railroaded if she's innocent."

"Hell, Adam, I don't want to see that, either. But *I'm* 'not wanting' it from a chair by the wall, instead of wearing a path in the floor. You wanna join me, or would you rather keep the boys in the other room guessing?"

Adam glanced through the glass. Several rangers quickly looked away and made themselves busy, but it was obvious they'd been watching him. Probably found it interesting that the brother of a local sheriff was so wrought up about their number-one suspect in a murder. A big murder. The murder of a Texas millionaire.

"Do you think she did it?" Adam asked his brother, ignoring the speculative eyes in the next room, carefully avoiding Garrett's question as well as his implication.

"Hell, no," Garrett answered without missing a beat. Then he frowned. *"Do you?"*

Adam didn't think she'd done it, but he wasn't sure if that was because he knew her so well, and knew she was incapable of murder, or because he was believing what he wanted to believe. He didn't quite trust his judgment where Kirsten was concerned. After all, he'd been pretty damned wrong about her once before.

About as wrong as a man could be.

"Do you?" Garrett persisted.

"Hell, I don't know what to think."

"Shoot, Adam, you know damn well Kirsten would never kill anybody." Garrett sounded as if he were heading into his big-brother mode. A lecture might follow any minute now. He'd taken on the role of father figure pretty seriously all those years ago. On that day that still haunted Adam the way it haunted them all. The day seventeen-year-old Garrett Brand had to tell his kid brothers and his baby sister that their mama and daddy wouldn't be coming home anymore. He'd done a hell of a job, keeping them together. Raising them. Running the ranch. A hell of a job. And if he still saw himself as the Brand patriarch, even now that his siblings were all grown up, that was fine by Adam.

But he could do without one of Garrett's lectures just now. "Do you think they'll arrest her?" He asked the question partly because he knew it would distract his brother. Mostly, though, he wanted to know. The thought of Kirsten behind bars bothered him more than it ought to. A lot more.

"Not just yet. They'll run the bullet through ballistics first, check out Cowan's will, question the household staff. They'll want to be sure they have a solid case before they charge her with anything. Hell, she might just be the richest woman in the county before too long. They won't want to make any mistakes on this one.''

"Unless she was telling the truth about the will," Adam said. Garrett led him toward the row of chairs, and Adam reluctantly sat down. "Why would he write his own wi—" Adam choked on the word, drew a breath, started over. "Why would he write her out of his will, Garrett?"

"I don't have a clue." Garrett looked him straight in the eye. "And I don't think you're doin' yourself any good by speculating on that. Or even by being here, for that matter. Why don't you go on home, Adam?"

It was a damned good question. Adam just shook his head. "I can't."

"Do I want to know why?"

"Hell, Garrett, *I* don't know why."

Garrett sighed in a way only a worried older brother could manage. "I just hope you know what the hell you're doing."

"I always know what I'm doing, don't I?" Right. He never acted without a plan. Without a reason. Without a clear goal in mind, and a set plan to go about achieving it. He'd wanted a wife, a life in Texas and enough capital to buy a ranch of his own and convert it into the dude ranch he and Kirsten used to dream of. He'd used his gift with numbers to get a degree, used the degree to get decent-paying jobs at local banks, and used the jobs to put aside the money for the ranch. He'd wooed and won the girl of his dreams, set the wedding date and they'd been well on their way.

Kirsten had tossed an unforeseen curveball at him by not showing up for the wedding. It had thrown him for a loop, but he'd recovered. His goals had changed, though. He'd decided he didn't want a wife or a dude ranch anymore. He wanted to get as far from Texas as possible, and he wanted to make a lot of money. And he set about doing both those things.

But the money hadn't made him feel any better about being jilted for a rich old man. And being in New York had served only to disconnect him from his family—his lifeline. So, a few minor adjustments and he was home again. And his goals were again altered. He was going to stay in Quinn and start his own business. Not a dude ranch, because that had been foolish from the start. A nice safe business, financial planning. He would be a consultant. He would continue making large sums of money, but he would do it right here in Kirsten's face. Not that her proximity had any bearing on it. And while he was at it, he would prove to his family—to this entire town—that he was over her.

And maybe he would prove it to himself while he was at it.

He didn't suppose being here with her right now was doing a hell of a lot to further either of those last two goals, was it?

His brother's hand landed heavily on his shoulder. "You want some more coffee?"

Adam glanced at the crushed foam cup in his clenched fist. "I think I've had a gallon already. And the stuff is like battery acid.'' Sighing, he glanced at the door. ''How much longer can they possibly keep her in there?''

The door opened, as if in answer to his question. Adam met Kirsten's eyes and felt that mule kick him in the gut once again. She looked all in. Her face was damp, and her sweat had thinned the makeup out so he could see through it now, to the paleness of her skin. A few tendrils of her doe-brown hair stuck to her forehead, and there was a wide, scared sort of look about her eyes. The cool, collected rich-bitch routine had vanished like a dandelion seed in a stray breeze. He glanced down at her hands automatically. Limp at her sides. Lifeless. At least they weren't sporting a pair of steel cuffs.

''I'll bring you a copy of Joseph's will this afternoon, Ranger Evans,'' Hawkins was saying. ''I only wish my memory were better, so I could have simply told you what was in it. But it has been some time since I've examined that particular document.''

The ranger looked skeptical. ''Don't leave town, Miz Cowan,'' he said. ''We'll be wanting to talk to you again real soon.''

''I can hardly wait,'' she said, her words cool, icy, despite the heat in the room. Surprising, that sharp tone, coming from a woman who looked as wrung out as she did. Maybe she didn't realize that her disguise had melted away. Maybe she thought she still looked the part. But she didn't. And the bite to her words got lost in the vulnerability of her face.

Adam moved toward her, responding to that vulnerability the way he always had.

She held up a hand and stopped him cold. "No. Stephen is driving me home. Thank you both for coming and waiting and…everything. But I'll be fine."

Right. And pigs would fly. Adam spoke without forethought. "You can't seriously think I'm going to…*we're* going to let you go back to that mausoleum alone," he said.

She turned her frosty gaze on him—or tried to. But it wasn't quite all snow and ice anymore. It was exhaustion, emotional and physical. And fear and uncertainty. Maybe even a hint of desperation. And for the first time, Adam thought maybe the rest of it was all just one big act. What if it was? Not just now, but all the time? What if she hadn't really changed at all deep down inside, underneath the polish and the ice?

"That's *exactly* what I think," she said in answer to his question. "I haven't been charged with anything, and I have every right to go home if I want to."

"Not alone."

She met his gaze, held it. Hers wavered first, and she lowered her head. "Alone is something I need right now. Try to understand that, would you, Adam? I've just lost my husband."

The barb sank deep. Like a hot brand in his chest. He didn't think he flinched, but he might have. Just for an instant he let those words hurt. But the hurt didn't stop him from replying, logically, calmly. "The killer could come back."

"He's right, Kirsten," Garrett interjected. "You *are* the only one who saw him."

"I couldn't identify him if he were standing in front of me," she said. "I told you, he had a mask...and the police have his gun. I'll be perfectly safe."

"You're right," Adam said. "You will."

Garrett searched his face. So did Kirsten. But he said no more. He just tipped his hat her way and headed out of the place.

Chapter 3

Kirsten didn't like it. She mulled over Adam's strange behavior all the way back to Quinn. But as she rode beside Stephen Hawkins in the comfortable leather seat of his car, she had no idea what to make of it. She only knew Adam was up to something, and she didn't like it one bit. She'd ripped the man's life to shreds twice now. For crying out loud, hadn't he had enough? Well, he wasn't going to get dragged into this mess. He wasn't. She wouldn't let him. Not this time.

"I have something to tell you," the aging attorney said softly. "And I'm afraid it isn't good news, Kirsten."

Stephen Hawkins drove too slowly. Then again, driving fast had been one bad habit she'd broken long ago. Not in time, though. Maybe creeping home at a snail's pace was some not-so-subtle reminder from the great beyond of what had gotten her into this nightmare to begin with. A reminder that if she did wind up serving a life sentence for murder, it would be no more than she deserved.

God, the irony was almost laughable.

"Kirsten?"

"Yes." She turned in her seat to face the older man. "I heard you. What is it?"

"It's about...Joseph's will."

She almost sighed in relief. "Don't worry, Stephen. I know he didn't leave me anything. I honestly never expected him to."

Stephen's Adam's apple swelled when he swallowed. "I wish...that were true. Kirsten, I lied to the rangers back there. I thought...well, I thought you might need some time. And that maybe within a day or two, other clues might surface...clues pointing to someone else. But I'm going to have to let them see Joseph's will, and I'm afraid that when they do..." His voice trailed off. He focused on the road and shook his head slowly.

"When they do...what?"

"Kirsten...Joseph came to me a month ago...to change his will."

She blinked. "Change it...in what way?"

"He named you his sole heir. You get everything, Kirsten. The estate. The holdings. All told...around twenty-three million in assets, give or take—"

"That's not possible." She stared at Stephen's profile, the sagging skin under his jaw, the honest blue eyes. "Stephen, he wouldn't...why the hell would he? He detested me!"

"He was a fool," Stephen said. "Maybe he realized that...decided to try to make up for—"

"Bull! My God, it's as if that bastard is reaching out from beyond the grave. As if he's trying to pull me down with him." She pressed her hands to her temples as tears stung at her eyes. "When they see the will, they'll have their motive, won't they, Stephen? They'll arrest me, charge me with murder. Won't they?"

He licked his lips. "Not...necessarily. The gun might provide evidence that someone else was responsible for Joseph's death. And the forensics team will have gone over the house by now. They may have found something there that..." He didn't finish. His words held little conviction.

Kirsten watched the mansion come into view long before they neared the driveway, rising up on the horizon like a dragon. And the gate, tall and iron and so pretentious with its gothic *J* on one side and the matching *C* on the other. The black gate was like a set of prison bars to her. The paved private lane that wound through it and up to the house, a path of despair. Even the tall, steep-roofed garage beside the place looked grim to her embittered eyes. Room enough for Joseph's small fleet of cars in the bottom, and a huge, luxurious apartment for his driver on the second floor. She ought to burn it all to the ground. She *hated* this house. It had been no more than a glittering, gleaming prison to her. She glanced again at

Stephen. "What do *you* think?" she asked, for some reason driven to know. "Do you think I did this—shot Joseph?"

"Of course not."

But he said it too quickly. And she didn't think she believed him. And then she knew she didn't when he added, "And to tell you the truth, Kirsten, if you had, I wouldn't blame you for it."

She closed her eyes. He thought she'd done it. Not for the money, but because he knew what a bastard Joseph had been. Most people knew that about him. So who the hell was going to believe her?

Only one person that she could think of. And she couldn't depend on Adam Brand to help her through this.

Adam and Garrett crossed the wide front porch, walked through the creaking screen door and were promptly met by three pairs of curious eyes and a barrage of questions. Ben, as big as Garrett, was typically quiet. His eyes spoke his concern for his brother, and a big hand on Adam's shoulder said he would help if he could.

A long time ago, Ben and Penny, and Adam and Kirsten had been a foursome. Inseparable. Things had changed. Adam was still as close to his brother as ever, and he loved Ben's wife, Penny, like a sister. But Kirsten had become his worst enemy. Penny still loved her, though. Ben, too, in his big, gentle way. Penny's eyes were red rimmed now, her voice soft.

"Is it true, Adam?" she asked. "Where is Kirsten?

I've been calling all day, but there's been no answer. Is she okay?''

Adam looked at Garrett, sent him an unspoken plea. He didn't want to go over all this again. Not now.

''I'll fill you all in,'' Garrett said, not letting him down. None of his brothers would ever let him down. If there was one thing he could depend on, it was that simple fact. Garrett sent Adam a nod, telling him to go on, do what he had to. Adam had a feeling his brother already knew what that was.

Adam started across the room, heading for the stairs as Garrett spoke. ''Kirsten's fine. Shaken, but fine. For now. She might be a suspect in Cowan's murder, though. She's been at the rangers' station in El Paso most of the day, but she's home now and—''

''I'm going over there,'' Penny interrupted.

That stopped Adam in his tracks. He spun around even before Garrett could speak. ''I don't want you going anywhere near that place, Penny.''

''She's my best friend, and she needs me.''

''And there's a killer on the loose. Ben, don't let her go over there.''

Ben frowned at his brother but knew better than to mistrust him. ''Honey, if Adam thinks it's dangerous…'' he began.

''Well, if it's dangerous for me, then what about Kirsten? Somebody ought to be over there watching out for her. She shouldn't even be there, for the love of heaven! I have to go. She'll listen to me.''

Ben stroked his wife's hair. ''Hey, slow it down, will you? I lost you once, honey, and I'm damned well not going to risk losing you again.'' He pressed one hand to her slightly expanded belly. ''And you have the baby to think about now, too.''

She pressed her lips together as Garrett and Chelsea both chimed in, backing Ben up one hundred percent. ''But what about Kirsten?'' she asked.

Adam sighed heavily. ''I've got that covered, hon.''

All three of them stared at him as if he'd grown another head, while Garrett just sighed as if he'd been expecting this.

''Adam, do you really think that's the best idea?'' Ben asked. ''One of us could probably handle watching out for Kirsten for a few days while all this sorts itself out. I could go over right now, and—''

''Right. Look, Ben, you have the martial arts school and a pregnant wife. Garrett's got the ranch to run, and with just him and Elliot to do it, he can't spare the time. Not to mention his duties as sheriff. Wes is busy with the mares about to foal, and Jessi and Lash are whooping it up with the big mouse in Orlando. I'll handle it.''

He turned again.

As he headed up the stairs, he heard Ben very softly asking Garrett, ''What the hell is up with him?''

''Your guess is as good as mine,'' was Garrett's soft-spoken reply.

Then Chelsea sighed and whispered, ''I sometimes think you Brand men are awfully slow on the uptake. I've gotta go call Jessi and tell her she was right all along. That chapter really *wasn't* over.''

Oh, but she was wrong, Adam thought. If she was

talking about the chapter in Adam's life that involved a relationship between him and Kirsten, she was dead wrong. He would go over there, and he would watch over her whether she liked it or not. Because he felt he ought to. Because if he got a phone call tomorrow saying she'd been murdered in her sleep, he would have to live with it, knowing he could have prevented it and hadn't. And because maybe this was the only way he would ever prove to himself and to everyone else in this family—in this entire town—that he was over her. Over her. Once and for all.

He'd finally figured out what his sorry mind had been lacking all this time where Kirsten was concerned. Closure. Maybe this was his chance to have it. Maybe in the process of getting her out of this mess, he would have time to make her answer the questions he'd never asked her. The questions he'd been avoiding all this time. Get that finality he needed to close her out of his soul for good. And she would give him the answers, too. Hell, she owed him that much. Yes, he thought. She owed him.

Kirsten's shaky grip on control broke down as soon as she closed the door of the mansion on Stephen and watched him walking back to his car. The shaking came first. Then the chills, and, finally, the tears. They were loud, and they were ugly. But for once it didn't matter. There was no one here to witness her falling apart.

Don't leave town. We'll be wanting to talk to you again, real soon.

She told her mind to be silent, and she headed for the stairs, sobbing hard, barely able to see through the blur of the tears in her eyes. A good thing, too, she thought as she moved through the huge house, because the study doors were open, and she didn't want to see what was in there. The blood on the floor. The marks of her bare feet drying in it.

But the images kept replaying over and over again in Kirsten's mind as she ran to her room, closed the door behind her and brushed the wetness from her face. She dragged a suitcase from under the bed, opened it, then went to the closet.

He changed his will, Kirsten. Named you his sole heir.

"Shut up!" She rapidly tossed clothes onto her bed.

Don't leave town....

As if they really expected her to sit here, just sit here, waiting for them to show up at the door with an arrest warrant. She didn't know how, she didn't know why, but somehow Joseph was responsible for this. All of it.

And he was thorough. If he wanted her destroyed, she would be destroyed. There would be no stopping whatever hideous wheels the bastard must have put into motion. He was capable of anything. *Anything.* She was scared. She was as scared as she'd been at fourteen when she'd first met Joseph Cowan, right after the horrible accident she'd caused. Joyriding in her daddy's car without permission. Without a license. Without a freaking *brain!* The one stupid, foolish act that had sealed her fate for good.

Joseph Cowan had *owned* her, body and soul, from that day on, even though she hadn't known it then. She hadn't known it until her wedding day, years later. Or…it would have been her wedding day. But the bastard had shown up to claim what she'd unwittingly sold to him long ago. Just like Satan claiming a damned soul.

She had to run.

"Kirsten?"

She spun so fast she almost fell over her feet. Adam Brand stood in the bedroom's doorway, looking from the pile of clothes on the bed to the open suitcase beside them…then focusing on her face. That was when his expression changed. His brows went up, and his lips thinned. She turned away fast. "I told you to stay away from me, Adam. I meant it."

"Yeah. I remember. You also told me you were fine, but you look like you just picked a fight with a hurricane and lost. So I'm thinking maybe you're not so fine, after all."

"It's none of your business, Adam."

"It is if you're planning to skip town," he said. "That *is* what you're planning, isn't it?"

She straightened, but didn't face him. Instead she strode into the bathroom, leaned over the sink and cranked on the water. She didn't bother closing the door. He would come in if he wanted to. He had obviously made quick work of the locks on the doors downstairs. Or had she even thrown them?

"Kirsten, you don't have to run. We can figure this out."

Bending over, she splashed water on her face. Then she lathered a cloth with cleansing lotion and began to scrub. Nobody was going to look at her with Tammy Faye streaks running over her cheeks, no matter what the circumstances might be.

"Figure *this* out, Adam. The bastard left me everything he had. And the minute the cops learn that, I'll be taken out of here in handcuffs. I don't plan to wait around for them."

Adam stepped right into the bathroom. She heard his booted footsteps, and when she reached for the towel, he handed it to her. "So you lied about the will?"

"No, I didn't lie about the freaking will. He changed it." She snatched up a brush and began tugging it through her hair.

"I see."

"You don't see a damn thing, Adam Brand. Go home. Leave me alone."

"I'm afraid I can't do that."

She paused with the brush in midair. "Why the hell not?"

"Because my brother gave the rangers his word he'd see to it you didn't leave town. He trusted you not to make a liar out of him, which is, apparently, just what you're about to do."

She drew a deep, calming breath. Time to lie. And she'd better make it good. It shouldn't be hard. Hell, she'd had years of practice. "I wasn't leaving town. Just this house." She finished her brushing, set the brush down and reached for the makeup case she kept in there. "I decided you were right about it not being safe. I thought I'd go to a hotel."

"Come to the ranch." He said it so fast she wasn't even sure he'd planned to.

"You've got to be kidding."

"No. Actually, the more I think about it, the better the idea seems. Penny's worrying herself sick about you, chomping at the bit to get over here—"

"You keep her away from here, Adam."

She stilled then. Because she'd whirled on him and gripped his arm, and she hadn't meant to. Closing her eyes, she relaxed her grip, but not before she felt his warmth, the tensing of his biceps, the shiver of awareness that moved through him. And something familiar, something precious, shimmered through her body and her mind. It left her shaken. She let go of him, but her hand still tingled with warmth and awareness. "I don't want Penny getting involved in this mess."

"I told her pretty much the same thing."

She swallowed hard. "If I go to the Texas Brand, I'll be dragging all this trouble there with me."

"We've done trouble before," he said. "We can handle it."

"Well I can't. It's bad enough I have to live through it. I'm not going to drag you...and Chelsea and little Bubba and Penny...no. I can't go to the ranch with you, Adam. And to tell you the truth, I'm a little surprised you even asked."

"To tell you the truth, so'm I." He shrugged. "Okay, then, what hotel?"

Frowning until her brows touched, she searched his face. *"What?"*

"What hotel?" he repeated. "Better call, tell 'em to make it a double room. Two beds."

"For God's sake, Adam, you can't possibly think you're going with me."

"If I'm not going with you, then you aren't going." He crossed his arms over his chest and leaned against the door frame.

Sighing, she lowered her head. "Okay. Okay, I'll bite. I have to admit, you've got me damned curious. Why are you doing this, Adam?" When he didn't answer, she lifted her head again, met his eyes. "You hate me for what I did to you. And you have every right to. You ought to be crowing like a rooster to see me finally getting my just deserts."

He drew a deep breath that made his chest expand, then blew it all out again. "Maybe I should. But I'm not. Nobody deserves this."

"You don't know the half of what I deserve," she said slowly.

"No? Well, I know a couple of things. You didn't shoot Joe Cowan."

It felt so good to hear those words—someone actually believing her, after facing the skepticism in the faces of everyone else she'd seen today. Every cop who'd questioned her. Even her own lawyer. She almost melted on the spot. And then he went on.

"And you didn't marry him for the money, either."

She went still. "How do you know that?"

"Because up until today, you thought you weren't

getting a dime of it. I know you well enough to know when you're lying, hon. And I don't think you were lying when you told me and Garrett that. So the big question on my mind is, why *did* you marry him?''

She shook her head, faced the mirror, fumbled in the makeup bag and pulled out some powders and brushes.

Adam came closer and stood behind her, hands on the back of her chair, looking at her in the mirror. She couldn't look back at him, and she dusted makeup over her face as fast as she could.

''What made you decide not to show up for our wedding, Kirsten?''

''You shouldn't ask a question like that, Adam. Because you sure as hell don't want to hear the answer.''

''I think I do. I think I *need* to hear the answer. So go on. Give it to me, Kirsten. I'm a big boy. I can take it.''

She still didn't meet his eyes. ''I'm not going to discuss this with you.''

''Did you love him?'' The question seemed to have been tugged out of him almost against his will.

She flinched when he asked it. She could pretend all she wanted. She could hide the truth and keep her secrets better than anyone she knew. But there was no way in hell she could look Adam Brand in the eye and tell him that she'd loved another man. A man she'd hated with every breath she drew. She couldn't do that. So she pressed her lips together and tried to pretend he wasn't there. She focused on her own reflection in the mirror, and slowly, methodically, she put her mask on and hid her dark truth away from those prying blue eyes.

Adam watched her face. It was amazing, the transformation. Her hands flew from one brush to another, and bit by bit the woman he remembered, the woman he'd loved, disappeared. She literally painted a new woman over her. She didn't answer his question. Not until she looked as if she had just stepped off the cover of some businesswoman's magazine. Not until she gathered her beautiful brown hair up into a tight little knot and stuck pins into it so viciously it seemed as if she were stabbing the old Kirsten to death in the process. Not until she'd sprayed it stiff, and he'd had to turn his head to get a breath of air that didn't choke him.

When she faced him again, she was the ice queen he hated. Not the vulnerable girl in the fight of her life who needed him. And she said, "I had my reasons for marrying Joseph. And none of them are any concern of yours."

"Did you love him?" he asked her again. He knew the answer before he asked the question. The woman sitting there with her painted-on face was incapable of loving anyone. But the girl underneath *had* been... once. Was she still?

"I really think," she said, rising slowly from her little stool like a phoenix from the ashes—transformed, strong, stubborn—"one interrogation a day is more than enough for me."

He only nodded. But he'd thought of something, and he couldn't stop until he probed just a little deeper.

"How's your father, Kirsten?"

She went utterly still. A doe caught in somebody's high beams. She blinked, averted her eyes. So she was still as firmly, even wildly, devoted to her father as she had always been. It was one of the things he'd loved best about her. And he'd never understood how even that could have changed. How she could have shipped him off to a home when she'd vowed to keep him with her always, no matter what. She'd even made it a condition when she'd accepted Adam's marriage proposal. She would marry him only if her father would always have a home in their household.

"Is he still in that nursing home in Dallas?" he asked her.

She nodded, her motions jerky as she turned her back to him and pretended to straighten the colorful containers and tubes on the countertop. "It's the best facility in the state." Her hands were shaking. The makeup stood in neat rows when she finished.

"I always wondered why you decided to ship him out there. I mean, it's not like there wasn't plenty of room right here. And God knows, you could have paid for a nurse to come in."

She stilled again, her head bent, her back still toward him. "Don't you dare question my love for my father, Adam Brand."

"I'm not questioning it. But I imagine he is."

She whirled, her hand slamming across his face so fast and so hard that he rocked back on his heels. He felt the sting. The surprise. Saw the fresh tears welling in her eyes. Felt an odd surge of relief that her feelings for her father hadn't turned to ice like everything else about her seemed to have done.

"I'd die for my father, you son of a bitch. He's where he is because it's the best place for him to be. And it's a good thing he is, because a shock like Joseph's murder would probably have killed him."

Adam stood there and saw raw honesty in her eyes, blazing bright. It was good to see it there for a change, instead of all those deceitful shadows he'd been trying to see past all day. "His heart's still that weak, is it?"

"His heart is shot," she said slowly, a little of the anger fading, a little of the stiffness easing from her body. "He's been on the transplant list for over a year now."

That knocked the wind out of his sails. Adam swore softly. "I didn't know. I'm sorry. I shouldn't have said what I did."

"No," she said. "You shouldn't have."

He drew a breath and sighed, not knowing what the hell to say or do next.

"I've changed my mind," she said finally. "I'm not going to a hotel. I'm going to stay right here. You can go home, Adam."

He shook his head. "Wish I could oblige you, Kirsten. But I can't. If you're staying here, I'm staying, too. I'll try to stay out of your hair."

"I suppose I could call the rangers and have you thrown out."

"I suppose you could. But you know damned well I'd only come back."

She stood glaring at him. He held her gaze with barely an effort. Looking into her eyes was like staring at a jigsaw puzzle and trying to find the missing pieces. He had a feeling he could look forever and not see everything going on inside her. Finally she sighed in defeat.

"Fine. Get the hell out of my room, then. Leave me alone."

He nodded. "I'll do that," he said. "But one word of warning, Kirsten. Don't try to leave this house. If you do, I'm gonna know about it, I promise you that."

She narrowed her eyes. He could see her wondering just what the hell he meant by that. But she didn't ask. It would only prolong this conversation, and it looked as if she was too relieved to finally see an end to it within reach. "Just go. Just get out of here and leave me alone, will you please?"

He gave a brief nod, turned and walked out of the bathroom, through the bedroom and out the door.

Kirsten followed him. She closed the door behind him, and he heard the lock turn. He stood there for just a moment, shamelessly listening, waiting.

Soft sobs came through loud and clear. And then another sound. The sound of liquid being poured into a glass.

Chapter 4

He shouldn't have made the remarks he had about her father. He had hurt her. But he'd learned something. She loved Max as much as she ever had. And her dad would have been living with her if it had been possible. Adam figured Max Armstrong might really be too weak to be out of the home, but on the other hand, that might not be the case. There might be some other reason why Kirsten hadn't wanted her father here with her. Adam intended to look into that—see if he could find out what the reason might be.

He tried to remember the name of the facility where Max Armstrong had been shipped right around the time of Kirsten's elopement. He'd heard it once. It would come to him. Meanwhile, he reprogrammed the security codes on the alarm system. He hadn't been bluffing. He would know about it the second Kirsten opened a door or a window. Or the second anyone else did.

When that was finished, he headed to the kitchen. Not that he gave a damn or anything, but Kirsten was running on empty. He hadn't seen her put a crumb of food into her mouth all day. She needed to eat or she would be in trouble. And he was so hungry his stomach thought his throat must have been cut, so he figured he might just as well fix enough for two.

The telephone shrilled while he stir-fried chicken and vegetables. This kitchen had everything—including an extension. But he ignored it, figuring Kirsten would prefer to get her own phone calls. Only when she hadn't answered on the fourth ring did he get nervous. Where the hell was she?

He snatched up the phone and barked an impatient "Yeah?"

There was a brief pause. Then, "Who is this? Where's Kirsten?" The voice was belligerent—and male.

"This is Kirsten's bodyguard," Adam sort of lied. "And she's busy. Who's calling?"

"Phillip...Mr. Cowan's driver."

Former driver, Adam thought, unless you've got a hearse handy. "She won't be needing you tonight," he told the man instead.

"Is she all right?" The man on the phone drew a breath. "Look, I heard about what happened, and I'm concerned about her being there alone...."

"Yeah, well, that's why I'm here. Believe me, pard,

no one's gonna get near her tonight. So you can quit worrying.''

"Oh. Well, that's...reassuring.''

"I'll bet. You and she have something going on?''

There was a series of half-blurted words followed by an indignant "Of course not!''

"Just curious,'' Adam said, not sure he believed the guy.

"Joseph Cowan has been like a father to me,'' the man said. "My God, I've been with him since I was—'' He broke off there.

"Go on. Since you were...?''

"It's none of your business. Are you some kind of cop, or...?''

"Where are you calling from, Phil?''

"It's Phillip. And I've already explained all this to the police. I've been out of town for several days. This was my week off.''

"Sounds like a solid alibi,'' Adam said. "I'm sure the rangers will verify it.''

"I imagine they're doing it as we speak,'' he replied, seemingly unruffled. "I didn't even know about...about Mr. Cowan's death...until they contacted me here to question me.'' He sighed, and the breath was broken, as if he really were grieving over this—or over something. "But I'm coming back right away, of course.''

"Of course. Look, I'm kinda busy here. Anything else I can do for you?''

"No. I'd just...I'd feel better if I could speak with Kirsten directly,'' Phillip said.

"Yeah, well, I'll pass that along." The hell he would. "If she feels like it, she'll call you when you get back. I'm afraid that's the best I can do."

"All right," Phillip said softly. "All right."

Adam hung up the phone.

So what was up with the driver? His interest had seemed more than casual, that was for sure. Sighing, Adam dropped a cover on the pan, turned the burner off and headed out to find Kirsten. If she'd been in her room she would have answered the damned phone. Wouldn't she?

The good thing about not drinking often was that it took very little time and effort to get completely blasted. By the second shot of Jack Daniel's, she felt the frayed edges of her nerves begin to smooth out. After she downed the third her lips were starting to go numb. Always a good sign.

She poured a fourth. She didn't want to think about anything. Not the fact that a killer was on the loose, or that she was probably going to end up in prison soon. Or that the man she loved—correction, the man she had once loved—hated her guts and was doing his best to torture her now. Or that she was a prisoner in her own home. She didn't want to think about her dad, either, sitting alone in that nursing home. Believing all the lies she'd told him...so many lies. He should have been here, with her. Adam was right about that. But she couldn't bring him. She couldn't. Seeing her with Joseph would have killed him. Her father knew her too well. He would have started figuring things out, and once he realized the truth…no, his heart never would have taken it. But God, now that Joseph was dead, she should be able to bring her father home. But she couldn't. How would he bear seeing her arrested and taken away in handcuffs? How could he survive a murderer skulking around the place? Not to mention finally learning the truth about all the lies she'd told.

No. It would have to wait. Just a little longer. She would find a way out of this. All she needed was one chance, one opportunity. She would get away, collect her father and head for the border. They could hide out in Mexico.…

Her glass was empty. She tipped the bottle to refill it, slopped the whiskey all over her hand, gave it up and took a slug from the bottle. Then she walked over to her dresser and pawed through the drawer full of designer swimsuits. She liked her white one best. Where was it? Oh, yeah, it was all bloodstained and stuffed into a plastic bag. The cops had taken it away. Shame, too. It was her favorite. She yanked out several, finally found the black one-piece with the zipper up the front, and then had to set her bottle down to get into it. It took longer than it should. She thought about doing without it, but decided that if the killer or the cops showed up, she would rather be dressed. Besides, Adam was still lurking around here somewhere, wasn't he?

She got the zipper tugged up, grabbed her bottle by the neck and took it with her. The hall floor wobbled a little, but she managed to grip the railing to keep her balance. She clung to it all the way down the stairs, and then turned and walked through the long corridor to the very back of the house, and through the big, ugly metal door there. This section housed the indoor pool, which was smaller and plainer than the one outside. Rectangular, Olympic sized. Not kidney shaped. No slides. Beyond the pool was the hot tub, situated in a glass alcove so one could get the feeling of being outside without the nuisance of mosquitoes or inclement weather. That Joseph had known how to live. The bastard.

She slipped into the hot bubbling water, hissing as she sank down until it reached her chin. Then she leaned back. Took another drink. There would be no hot tubs in prison. And if she ran to Mexico, she wouldn't be able to afford one. She'd best enjoy this while she could.

Kirsten was not in her room, or the bathroom attached to it. But her suitcase was back in the closet. Adam had taken a quick peek into the garage before coming up here, and both Cowan Mercedes were still in place. His own Jag sat outside, where he'd left it. So she must still be in the house.

He always operated with a careful plan, a well-thought-out goal and a means to achieve it. So what the hell was he doing here, playing baby-sitter to a murder suspect—one he detested? He'd given this no forethought. He had no plan. He'd acted on impulse. He had no idea what he was doing, where this was going, or what route it would take to get there. He was flying by the seat of his pants, and he didn't like it.

He glanced at the mess she'd made of her bedroom. A dresser drawer stood wide-open, its colorful contents spilling from it. Several bathing suits were scattered on the floor. The bed was rumpled, and the cabinet beside it stood open.

Frowning, he walked over to that cabinet, hunkered down and peered inside. A few bottles of expensive wine stood in a neat row, unopened. But there was an empty spot in the lineup. He closed the door and eyed the empty glass sitting in a puddle on the polished top of the bedside stand. Leaned closer and sniffed.

"Whiskey." He sighed. "Hell, I can't say as I blame her."

He glanced again at the bathing suits strewn about the floor, the prim white outfit she'd been wearing tossed carelessly down, as well. The pool? No. It was outside. She would have set off the alarm if she'd opened the doors. What else?

Damned if he knew. Maybe she had a tanning salon hidden in this monstrosity somewhere. Sighing, Adam resigned himself to a long search. But it ended up being a lot shorter than he'd expected. Because as soon as he headed back downstairs and started moving through the house, calling her name, he heard her off-key singing echoing through the place.

And for just a second, he smiled. Damn. Kirsten had always loved to sing. The problem was, she usually sounded like a wounded coyote, and that was sober. Right now her imitation of Celine Dion would have brought tears to the superstar's eyes. But at least it guided him to where she was.

He found her in a huge room at the rear of the house with skylights, a big pool and a gigantic hot tub surrounded on three sides by glass walls that looked out onto a starry Texas night. The ceiling directly above the hot tub was glass, too. Kirsten's arms were stretched to either side and resting on the marble edge. She held a nearly empty JD bottle in one hand. Her head was tipped back, her eyes were closed and she was bellowing to the heavens. By all appearances, she was well and truly snockered.

Adam walked over to the hot tub and waited for her to run out of wind on the closing note—if it could be called a note. She did, finally. Lowered her head and opened her eyes to look directly at him.

"Found me, huh?"

"Looks like. So how drunk are you, hon?"

"Not drunk enough." She looked at her empty bottle with regret. "Sorry, I didn't save you any."

"Well, maybe I'd best stay sober tonight." He glanced at her hands. "Your fingers are starting to prune up. You think you've been in there long enough?"

She shrugged.

"I made you some dinner. Come on." He held out a hand.

She didn't take it. "I love my father, you know," she said.

Adam swallowed hard. "So you've been sitting here getting drunk and thinking I don't know that?"

She looked up at him. Big eyes, totally without pretense now. Her makeup had washed off in the water.

Her face was as naked and as honest as he'd ever seen it, and he liked it that way.

"I know you love Max. I shouldn't have said what I did."

"I had to take him to Sunnyside. I had to." She shook her head, shot him a look. "You think I would have taken him there if I'd had a choice?"

Adam shook his head. "No, I know you wouldn't have. It's okay. C'mon, get out of the water now."

Kirsten shook her head. Her eyes were moistening, and her lower lip protruding a bit. She sniffed. "If he'd known what I did to you...if he'd known we never...and he was so sick anyway, just before the wedding. All the excitement, it was just too much for him."

Adam frowned at her. "Wait a minute. He was sick? That was why he never showed that day? I thought you must have just told him it was off...even though you never bothered to tell me."

He'd been truly worried when Max hadn't shown up...but not for long. Within minutes his worry had focused on Kirsten. And when he learned what she'd done, his worry had turned to rage.

"I took him to see Doc the day before," she said, speaking softly, as if she were thinking it all through in her mind and just saying it aloud to solidify the thoughts. "Doc said he ought to be in the hospital. Daddy...he said he'd go, but he made me promise to go ahead with the wedding anyway. Said it would kill him if he thought we'd postponed it because of him. So I just...I just let him think we..."

"You never told him the difference?" Adam said slowly. "I can't believe this. Your father thinks we've been married all this time?"

She closed her eyes, let her head rest on the floor behind her. "I couldn't tell him about Joseph. He hated Joseph. All his life, he hated him."

Adam hunkered down beside the hot tub, his curiosity piqued. "Why?"

Kirsten shrugged. "I don't know. But Joseph hated Daddy right back." She sat up, tipping her bottle to her lips, then frowning at it because it was empty.

"Come on. Out of the water," Adam said. He held out his hand once more. She set the bottle down and lifted hers. Adam clasped it. Cool and damp. Small and fragile. She got to her feet, and he steadied her up the marble steps, out of the water. She closed her eyes and breathed in slowly. Then she took her hand away. "I can manage by myself."

"Yeah, I can see that."

She thrust her chin out and strode forward—then her arms started wheeling as one foot slipped on the wet surface. He snagged her waist, but it was too late. She was going in, and she took him with her. They splashed into the hot tub. When Adam got himself upright, she was wrapped around him like a spider monkey. Legs locked around his waist, arms locked around his neck. His hands were on her backside, and he was damned if he knew how they'd gotten there. But it felt good. She felt good. Firm and tight, and she was pressing against him in all the right places, and he was hard and pressing back.

She looked up, wide-eyed, mouth slightly open.

"Oh, hell," he muttered, and he told himself this was the stupidest, most idiotic, poorly thought out invitation to disaster he'd ever issued…and then he kissed her. He just bent his head and pulled her harder against him, and gobbled up her wet mouth as if he'd been starved to death for it forever.

And it occurred to him that maybe he had been.

She tasted good. Warmth and whiskey on her tongue as he drew it into his mouth and sucked at the flavor. His hands tightened on her butt, and she pressed herself against him. He walked forward through the churning water until her rear end landed on the built-in bench, and then he brought his hand around between them and reached for his zipper.

She felt it, his knuckles between her legs. And she jerked her mouth away from his.

"What the hell are you doing?"

He blinked his eyes open. "I…"

"No way in hell, honey," she said, pushing herself up to the edge and scooting backward across the marble. "I'm not *that* drunk."

He got his breathing under control with an effort. "I'm not drunk at all. Sorry, Kirsty. I didn't mean for that to happen."

As he moved up the steps she was silent, staring wide-eyed, looking wounded, near tears. "What?" he asked. "What did I say?"

She closed her eyes tight, bit her lip. "Nothing. Maybe…something to eat wouldn't be a bad idea after all, huh?"

He lowered his head, ashamed of himself, shocked by the desire that had just rocketed through him so powerfully that all common sense had fled. For crying out loud, he was *over her.*

He was.

"So what did you make?"

He looked up at her again. A huge mistake, he thought. Because he couldn't keep his eyes on her face. Her bathing suit fit like a second skin, and that zipper was down low enough to reveal the smooth, round tops of her breasts. Her nipples showed right through the fabric. She sure as hell had kept herself in shape. She looked better than ever. And he wanted her. He might be completely over the emotions he'd once felt for her, but the physical part was even stronger than it had been before. Damn his body for craving hers like this.

"Adam?"

He swallowed hard. "Stir-fry," he muttered. "Chicken."

She nodded, staggered across the floor to a rack with towels hanging from it, reached for one and missed. Blinking slowly, she tried again, snagging a towel this time and half falling, half sitting on a bench to rub at her hair, and her face, and her arms. He wanted to do it for her.

Adam walked over, dripping dark-colored water. His clothes were not chlorine proof, then. Great. He snatched a towel of his own. "Hey, Kirsty, you'd best turn around, unless you want an eyeful. If I don't get out of this stuff, my skin's gonna be dyed to match my pants.''

Without looking at her to see if she'd obeyed, he shucked off the trousers, peeled off the shirt. Stood there in his dripping wet shorts and nothing else. When he started rubbing himself down, he glanced her way and figured it was a damned good thing he *hadn't* had any of that whiskey, because the way she was looking at him just then would have been too much to resist.

Maybe it was anyway.

He dropped the towel and took a single step toward her. Then he stopped himself. She was drunk. His daddy had never sired any son who would take advantage of a woman in the condition she was in right now. Especially after what she'd been through today. His mama would be ashamed of him if she could see him. And Garrett would knock him right square on his backside for even thinking about it. Garrett put a lot of stock in honor and chivalry and respecting a woman. Enough so that Adam knew better than to do what every cell in his body was screaming to do right now.

He licked his lips and turned away, knotted the towel at his hip to hide the bulge of his arousal. Didn't do a hell of a lot of good. Then he reached for her hand, pulled her to her feet. ''Come on. Let's find some dry clothes. Then we'll see if a plateful of food does anything to absorb all the whiskey in your belly.''

"Hell, it's all in my bloodstream by now, Adam. And I like it there."

He frowned at her, worried by those words. "Don't get to liking it too much."

"What difference would it make if I did? I'm only going to prison anyway."

"You think so?"

She shrugged as he led her back through the house. "That or Mexico."

"Why, Kirsten?" He watched her face, half expecting her to confess to murder, half praying she wouldn't.

"Because it's looking like that's what Joseph wants. And Joseph Cowan *always* gets what he wants."

Adam narrowed his eyes on her. What the hell did she mean? Did she think her husband was setting her up from beyond the grave? Hell, she was drunk. She wasn't making any sense, and he probably shouldn't pay a lot of attention to anything she might say.

"That's what he was always saying." They stopped outside the library, and she flung open the double doors and stood staring inside. Adam followed her gaze to the huge portrait of Joseph Cowan that hung on the wall above the fireplace.

"'Don't try to fight me, Kirsten,'" she quoted, mimicking Cowan's voice. "'I'm a powerful man. I always get what I want.'" Then she pressed a hand to her lips to stifle a bark of bitter laughter. "Well, guess what, you bastard. You didn't. Not *always*."

There were wet footprints throughout the house, and

more water dripped from Adam now, to puddle on the library floor. He secretly gloried in that.

"You didn't get a baby, did you, Joseph?" Kirsten suddenly cried. "And God knows you tried." She laughed again, but the sound was so anguished it was more like a cry. "You stupid old fool—on me all the time. Grunting and sweating until I thought your heart would give out. I hoped it would, I really did. Did you know that, Joseph? Did you know I was lying there wishing your heart would explode in your chest? Did you know how much I hated your hands on me? How I used to throw up when it was over? How I used to stay in the scalding shower until my skin was raw trying to wash your stench away? Did you!"

Adam felt his stomach convulse, and his entire body came alive with a painful rage. He touched her shoulders from behind. She shrugged his hands away. Fury seemed to emanate from her like a living force.

"You never knew about the birth control pills, did you, Joseph? I won that round. I won that round! It was all for nothing. I beat you, you son of a bitch."

"Kirsten…" Adam gripped her shoulders, spun her around and searched her face. He saw the hatred in her eyes. He didn't know what to say, what to think.

"Thank God he's dead," she murmured, and the tears welled. "Thank God he'll never put his despicable hands on me again." She fell against Adam, and he closed his arms around her.

A cold feeling infused his entire body, as if his blood had been replaced with snow and his heart with a hunk of ice. What in hell had she been through? And why? Why had she given herself to a man she obviously hated? Why had she married him?

He asked her.

But she didn't reply, and he realized her body had gone limp in his arms. He turned her face to his, looked down at her. Out cold.

Swallowing hard, Adam lifted her into his arms and carried her—not to the kitchen, as planned, but up the stairs and into her room.

He laid her down on the bed, with a towel underneath her so she wouldn't soak the covers through. Then he bent over her, reached for the zipper on her sexy little black swimsuit and slowly pulled it down.

Chapter 5

Adam stopped with her zipper in his hand. This was definitely not a good idea. "Hey, Kirsty. Come on, wake up." He shook her none too gently.

Her eyes opened and gazed myopically up at him. A silly, crooked smile twisted her lips. "You called me Kirsty again. I wish you'd stoppit."

A lump formed in his throat. "Sorry. It just slipped out." No one else had ever called her Kirsty and lived to tell about it. But when he'd done it, way back when, she'd liked it. Hell, there was a time when she'd pretty much liked everything he did.

But he wasn't going to think about that now. Not while he was standing over her bed, and they were both wet, and he was dressed in no more than a pair of damp shorts and a towel, thinking about undressing her. "Don't you have a maid or something?"

She blinked, bunched up her brows as if she were thinking very hard. "Nobody's comin' today. I told 'em not to bother."

"Well, you need to get into some dry clothes, and I'm the only one here to help."

She lifted her brows and looked up at him. No ice princess in sight. She looked worried.

"Unless you can manage by yourself."

"'Course I can." She sat up. Put her feet down. Braced her hands on the edge of the mattress and started to stand, then teetered and landed on the bed again. "Or maybe not."

"Just sit there," Adam said. "I'll find you some clothes."

He started off in one direction, but she pointed him in another. "In the closet, Adam. The big warm snuggly blue one." She hugged herself as she said it, and Adam guessed she didn't mean the big warm snuggly blue closet but something *inside* the closet.

He opened the door and found it. Hanging inside the door, a flannel nightgown somebody's granny ought to be wearing. "Perfect," he said. If he couldn't keep his thoughts in line when she was wearing that number, then he was beyond help. Taking it down, he turned, but before he handed it to her, he noticed that it was as soft as down and he ran his hands over the fabric, then closed his eyes, because even the granny gown now seemed somehow erotic to him. Man, he was one sorry pup.

She yanked down the zipper of her swimsuit. Then lifted her head and said, "Turn around."

He didn't know what kind of look she sent him, because his eyes were glued elsewhere. But he did tear them away and turn his back to her. Not that it did anything to erase the image from his mind. "Just, uh…holler if you need help."

"I been dressing myself all my…ouch!"

"Kirsty?"

"Stop saying that!"

He heard muffled cussing and the squeak of the bedsprings as she wrestled with her clothes. Eventually she said, "Okay."

He turned around. She had the nightgown on backward. His heart made a funny lump in his chest that felt a lot like a big lead ball of regret. He walked over to her and tugged her arms out of the sleeves without lifting the nightgown any higher than her knees. She sat just as docile as a lamb. He stood her up, turned the nightgown around and helped direct her arms back where they belonged. She grinned. "Thanks."

"Don't mention it."

"Did you say something about food earlier?"

"You think you can cling to consciousness long enough to eat it?"

She shrugged. Her eyes drooped. "Come on," he said, and he scooped her up. He didn't set her down again until they reached the kitchen. And by then her head was nodding toward his shoulder and resting there every few seconds. He put her in a chair. "Stay awake," he ordered.

She giggled. "You're still wearing that towel."

"Yeah. Hang in there a minute and I'll fix that."

He scooped the chicken and vegetables onto a plate, grabbed up a fork and set it all in front of her. "I won't bother heating it up. I doubt you'd notice, anyway."

She smiled and dug in. Chewed, licked her lips and started shoveling.

"I take it that means you like it?"

"Mmm," she said with her mouth full.

He poured her a glass of milk and placed it on the table. "Be right back." She only nodded and kept on eating, oblivious, he thought, to anything else.

Adam went to the foyer, where he'd dropped his overnight bag when he'd come in. Taking it to the nearest bathroom, he tossed on some dry clothes and carried the wet ones back into the kitchen with him. It took him only five minutes. But when he got back, it was to find Kirsten facedown on the table beside an empty plate and a drained milk glass. And he guessed she was down for the count this time.

"Come on, princess. Time for bed." He picked her up again. She was warm and totally limp in his arms. He carried her up to her bed, tucked her in and stationed himself in the overstuffed chair nearby. He didn't expect her to get up and go wandering off during the night—unless it was to the bathroom to lose her dinner. But he figured he'd best err on the side of caution as long as Joseph Cowan's killer was on the loose.

He would like to pin a medal on the guy who'd murdered the rich old bastard. But he would be damned if he let him get his hands on Kirsten.

Adam settled into the chair and tipped his hat down over his eyes. But sleep didn't come easy, and when it did, it was far from peaceful. He dreamed of Kirsten. Not the sophisticated rich man's wife, but the fun-loving girl he'd been hell-bent on marrying. Then he saw her lying on her back, eyes unblinking and cold, beneath that disgusting old man. He saw Cowan's hands on her. His mouth on her. Saw the light that used to be in her big brown eyes slowly die.

She'd never loved the man. She'd never loved *any* man but him. So why had she married Cowan? For the love of God, why?

Kirsten woke up and wondered why her mouth felt so dry and sticky. Then she moved, and her head swam and her stomach writhed. She slammed her eyes closed, because the brightness hurt. "Oh, God, I'm dying," she moaned.

"Nah. Just hung over."

She opened one eye. Adam stood beside her bed with a big glass of what looked like tomato juice in one hand. Damn, he was still here. "Why am I not surprised?" she muttered.

"Here. Drink this. Guaranteed cure for what ails you."

She took the glass, sat up *very* slightly, sniffed it. "What's in it?"

"That's a secret. Wes would shoot me if I gave away his recipe."

She blinked. Adam's brother Wes used to be a hel-lion. If anybody would know about curing a hangover, she would bet on him. "I don't usually drink something if I don't know the ingredients."

"Well, you knew the ingredients of that Jack Daniel's last night, and I don't see that it did you much good." She frowned at him. Her head throbbed. Adam went on. "'Course, if you'd rather feel like hell all day…"

She tipped the glass to her lips. It was good. Tasty and tangy, even though her stomach rebelled at the first swallow. She forced it down, motivated by the dim hope of relief. God, her head was spinning in the most sickening way.

She set the empty glass on the nightstand. And then realized she was wearing her favorite flannel granny gown and didn't remember putting it on. Uh-oh. Lifting her head slowly, she searched Adam's face for a telltale satisfied smile but saw no clue. "I…um… don't remember much that happened last night."

"We made out in the hot tub, and then I took you to bed."

"We…?"

He grinned and sent her a wink. He didn't look like a man who hated her guts. But she knew Adam too well to think he would have engaged in sex with a woman too drunk to know what she was doing. No way. The Brand boys had the market cornered on honor. It wasn't in him.

Odd that the one person she trusted pretty much unconditionally was the man she'd made into her worst enemy. The one she was lying to with every minute that passed without her telling him the truth.

She closed her eyes, searched her memory. Then they flashed wider. "My God, we *did* make out in the hot tub." She remembered it. She got hot remembering it. The feel of his mouth devouring hers, his hands on her, his body pressing into hers. She searched his face.

He shook his head. "Don't look so mortified, Kirsty. Nothing happened. Well, nothing much. I mean, I didn't...we didn't..."

"I know." She bit her lower lip. "Thanks. For being a gentleman."

"Yeah, whatever."

"And for the cure." She nodded at the empty glass. "I think I feel a little better."

"Up to company?"

She blinked fast, and her heart skipped. "The rangers are back? Already?"

Adam sat down on the side of the bed. There was an edginess about him this morning. A tightness to his jaw that hadn't been there even when he'd been in the full throes of hating her guts. What the hell had she said to him last night?

"No. You're scared to death, aren't you?"

She met his eyes, hated admitting to weakness, and nodded anyway. "It's tough wondering if they're going to come charging through the front door with a warrant for my arrest at any second."

Adam drew a breath, sighed. "Maybe I can help with that."

"How?"

"Well, my brother is the sheriff." He licked his lips, studied her eyes. "Tell you what. If you'll give me your word that you won't make a run for it...I'll ask Garrett to let us know if things progress that far."

She could not believe this guy. "You think he would do that? Warn us if the rangers decide it's time to place me under arrest?"

"He's my brother," Adam said, as if those three words not only answered the question but explained the answer, as well. "That way you know you'll have some advance warning. Time to prepare yourself. And you won't have to worry that they're going to show up at any time. Unless Garrett calls, you'll know they aren't going to show up at all."

She nodded, and another heavy weight seemed to be lifted off her shoulders. God, why was he helping her? Why was she *letting* him? Was it possible that Adam Brand still felt something for her?

Something *besides* plain old lust, which still flowed full force between them. They'd pretty much established that last night. But Adam *couldn't* feel anything beyond that. Not after all she'd done, and all this time. It made no sense. He hadn't felt that much for her to begin with. Oh, he'd said the words, walked the walk. But there had always been a part of himself that he held back. A part he couldn't share. A place she couldn't touch. She'd believed once that, given time, she would be able to reach that spot inside him. But she'd run out of time. And she could never get it back.

She blinked and brought herself back to the present.

"So if it isn't Officer Friendly and his paddy wagon, who is the company?"

"A pair of Brands. Ben couldn't keep Penny away. The quicker you see her, the quicker he can get her back to the ranch, where it's safe." He blinked. "If you were smart, you'd pack a bag and let me take you back there, as well, Kirsten."

"Yeah, well, I never claimed to be Einstein." She sat up, leaned over and rubbed her temples. "Go keep an eye on her, will you? Give them coffee or something. Buy me some time to…"

"Put the mask on?" he asked with a nod toward the vanity and the makeup scattered all over it. Then he turned back to her. "You don't need it anymore, Kirsty. Cowan is dead. It's just us here now. And there's nothing you need to hide from me."

He didn't have a clue to all the things she had to hide from him. She tried not to look scared. "Just buy me some time, would you?"

With a sigh, he nodded. Then he gave her one last searching glance, got to his feet and headed downstairs to join his brother and sister-in-law.

He was seeing too much. More than she wanted him to see. He'd already gotten past her icy-bitch persona and touched the woman she used to be, the one she'd thought was dead and buried. Nobody had ever been able to get to her the way Adam had. God, she'd loved him to utter distraction once.

She forced herself to get up, choose clothes. A cool frosty green sleeveless jumpsuit, white belt and flats. She laid them on the bed and took a five-minute shower. Then spent thirty more blow-drying and spraying and applying makeup. She didn't have time to do her nails, but yesterday's white polish didn't look too bad, and it matched. Little white pearls on her ears. Great. She glanced into the mirror. "The bitch is back," she muttered. But she wasn't. Not really. Her eyes were soft with something she really didn't like seeing in them. Something she didn't even dare analyze right now. She wasn't ready for what she was glimpsing hints of in her own eyes.

Kirsten found Penny pacing the living room, back and forth past the foot of the stairs, pausing every so often to glance up. Catching sight of Kirsten, she threw her arms open and raced up to meet her. That warm hug almost brought Kirsten to tears, but she hugged Penny back. Penny, the woman who'd been her best friend, then a total stranger who not only didn't remember her but mistrusted her, and finally her friend again, and closer than before. And even *she* didn't know the truth. Her husband, Ben, knew part of it…but not all. If he knew it all, he would hate her, too.

"Sweetie, are you okay? My God, it's terrible about Joseph."

Kirsten met her friend's eyes, glanced past her, didn't see Adam or Ben nearby. "You know things were bad between us, Penny. I'm not exactly broken up over his death. It's almost a relief."

"I know. I know, but…honey, you've got to be scared to death, staying here with a killer on the loose."

She shrugged. "Adam won't leave. I suppose I'm safe enough with him around."

Penny eyed her. "Yeah. I'm finding that one pretty puzzling myself."

"Tell me about it," Kirsten said. Then she had a thought that frightened her. "Where is he? With Ben?"

Penny nodded. "In the kitchen." And when Kirsten started to rush past her, Penny caught her arm. "Ben told me, Kirsten. About…about what you confided to him that night at the dojo. And I imagine by now he's told Adam, as well."

"No. He wouldn't have…he gave his word he'd keep it between us."

"Maybe he thinks the stakes are higher now than they were when he made that promise."

Kirsten sank onto the bottommost stair, lowering her head. "What…what did he tell you?" *What's he telling Adam?*

"He said you were blackmailed into marrying Joseph Cowan. That Joe had something on you, and that you were hoping to get something equally damaging on him and force him to let you go."

Kirsten closed her eyes, sighed deeply.

"You can't blame him for telling us. Honey, this could all be involved in what happened to Joseph. The truth is going to have to come out sooner or later."

"All the truth is going to do, Penny, is provide the police with yet another motive to add to the ever growing list of reasons why I might have murdered my husband."

Penny frowned at her. "Kirsten, none of us are going to pass this on to the police...."

"Penny, your brother-in-law *is* the police."

"And you're family," she insisted.

"No. I was never family."

Penny's eyes got misty. She closed a hand around one of Kirsten's. "You are to me."

Closing her eyes, Kirsten whispered, "Thanks for that."

"So, did you succeed? Did you ever get anything on Joseph?"

"No. If I had, I'd have been out of here by now. The man was as slippery as a snail. It was a stupid idea." She opened her eyes and stared at some invisible spot in midair. God, Adam was going to want to know what Joseph had used against her. She was going to have to tell him. She couldn't even imagine forcing the words through her lips. Telling the secret she'd given up her life—her very soul—to keep.

"Kirsten, if he would blackmail you, don't you think he might have used the same tactics with other people?" Penny was up, pacing now. The caring-sister routine falling beneath the onslaught of Penny Lane Brand, private eye. She'd been a Nancy Drew wannabe from the time she read her first mystery. And now that she was taking P.I. classes at the community college, she was damned dangerous. God help them all. "If we could find out for sure, that would give someone else a motive for murder and maybe help clear you."

Kirsten hit the Pause button on her inner turmoil

and shot her friend a look. "Did you get your P.I. license yet, Penny?"

With a sheepish smile, Penny shook her head. "I take the finals next week. But I can't go into business until after the baby comes. Wouldn't be safe."

"Won't be any safer then. And it isn't exactly safe to be hanging around here, either."

"Then why are you?"

Kirsten swallowed. She licked her lips. "I'm not dragging all this trouble with me to the Texas Brand, Penny. And I'm not bringing it to that nice house you and Ben built next door to the new dojo, either."

Penny tilted her head. "You know, when we rebuilt the dojo, we put an apartment above it. You could—"

"Right. And if the killer pops in during Ben's pre-school tai chi class, the four-year-olds will just drop-kick him."

Penny sighed. "There's just no talking to you, is there?"

Kirsten shook her head.

"Will you tell me what it was that Joseph had on you, Kirsten?"

Meeting her best friend's eyes, she said, "I'm sorry, Penny. But I can't."

"Okay," Penny said. She squeezed Kirsten's hand as Kirsten got to her feet. "Just remember, once it's told, it's not a secret anymore. And once it's not a secret, it loses its power."

A surge of heat and moisture welled up in Kirsten's eyes, and her throat went tight, just at the thought of telling Penny, or Ben...or Adam. God, he was the one who had suffered the most, wasn't he? Adam. He would never forgive her if he knew...and she realized now—as she had perhaps realized on some level all along—that he was going to have to know, sooner or later.

God, please, later.

She stepped into the kitchen with Penny at her side, and she saw him. He sat in a chair staring back at her, and it was in his eyes. Ben had told him what he knew. Thank goodness Ben didn't know all of it. There was an apology in Ben's eyes when they met hers. In Adam's there was only a question.

One she couldn't answer.

Because what could she say?

I'm really sorry, Adam. But it turns out I'm the one who killed your parents twenty years ago. I'm the one who orphaned six kids. I'm the reason your oldest brother Garrett had to give up his scholarship to college and take over running a ranch and raising a family at seventeen, and the reason your baby sister never knew her mother's love. And I'm the reason you can't love, Adam. Because you're so afraid of being abandoned again; of being hurt again the way you were when your big brother had to tell you that your mother and father wouldn't be coming home anymore. It was me. I killed your parents, Adam. And I can't tell you how many times I've wished it had been me instead of them.

Chapter 6

"Why didn't you tell me?"

Adam stood beside the front door, staring out the window at Ben's pickup as it moved down the endless driveway to pass through the gates to the road beyond. He didn't look at Kirsten. He didn't want to just now. He was too afraid of the powerful emotions swirling around inside him. Too afraid of losing control.

It had been bad enough trying to make sense of what she'd revealed last night, the sickening pictures she'd painted with her words...pictures of Cowan in her bed, in her body, when she didn't want him there. But now this. His brother's revelation that made it sound as if maybe she'd been forced into this marriage against her will. As if she'd had no choice.

"Why didn't you just freaking *tell me?*" he asked

her again. They seemed to be the only words that came
to him.

Kirsten lowered her head. "I couldn't. I still can't."

"The hell you can't." He did turn now. But she
looked into his eyes for only the briefest instant. Pain
flickered and died in hers, and then she just walked
away. Adam followed her back through the foyer and
into the opulent living room beyond, with its glittering
crystal chandelier and its velvet-trimmed wall cover-
ings and matching draperies and shiny marble floor
tiles. It looked like a funeral parlor.

"I think I have a right to know," he said.

She stopped walking, turned to face him. "It
doesn't matter anymore, Adam. It's ancient history."

"How can you stand there and say it doesn't matter? For crying out loud, woman, you'd be my wife
right now if that bastard…" He didn't finish, just
shook his head and searched her face. "What the hell
could he have had on you that was so bad it would
make you miss your own wedding day—would make
you leave the man you claimed to love standing alone
in a country church with half the town looking on?
Would make you send your own father away just to
keep him from learning the truth?"

She stood still, shook her head. "Adam, don't—"

He gripped her arms. "Not to mention making you
marry a man you didn't love."

She lowered her head, closed her eyes as if shutting
him out. "I had to do what I thought best at the time.
It's that simple. It was my life, Adam. My decision."

"It was *my life* that son of a bitch messed with.

And I want to know why.'' She looked up at him again and let him see inside her, just for a moment. He stared down into her eyes and saw more secrets there than he'd ever seen. And more than that, he saw her fear— fear that those secrets would be found out.

The doorbell broke the tension like a hammer on a sheet of glass. She pulled away, turned toward it.

"Don't," he told her.

She stopped, her back to him, her head hanging down. "You're right, Adam. You have a right to know. And I'll tell you…everything. But right now I can't. Because you'd have to tell your brother, and he'd be honor bound to tell everyone else.''

"Everyone else?''

"The Texas Rangers, the D.A., anyone else who's looking for one whopper of a motive for me to have murdered my husband. They'd have it, Adam. They'd have it in spades if they knew the truth. And I'd be convicted so fast there would barely be time to mount a defense.''

He lowered his head. "So it comes down to trust. And you don't have any in me.''

Her rigid stance wavered just a little. "You're the only person I do trust, Adam.''

He closed his eyes and moved forward almost against his own will. God, what she'd been through. It was killing him to know what she'd been through. His hands slid over her shoulders, and he pulled her back until her body rested against his. "I'm sorry, Kirsty.''

"For what?''

The doorbell chimed again. Adam ignored it. It crossed his mind that she might not even remember the things she'd blurted out last night, while she'd raged drunkenly against her dead husband. But he knew, and he couldn't forget. If it were true, if she'd been somehow forced into this marriage, then what Joseph Cowan had done to her had been rape. There was no other word for it, no softening of it. It had been rape.

But maybe it would be easier on her if she didn't remember her nighttime confessions.

"There's no reason for you to apologize to me, Adam. Nothing for you to be sorry for."

He shook his head. "There's a lot," he said slowly. "I'm sorry for not being there for you when you needed help. For leaving town in a jealous rage instead of sticking around to find out what was really happening. For the two years you spent married to a bastard…" His throat closed off. He couldn't go on. The images were back, torturing him. Burning themselves a home in his brain. Cowan. And Kirsten. Her eyes too cold to shed tears.

"None of that was your fault."

He didn't have time to answer. His brother Garrett's voice came thundering through the walls, calling Adam's name while beefy fists banged on the door. Hell, Garrett was probably worried half to death by now. Adam leaned forward and pressed a soft kiss to Kirsten's hair. "I'm gonna make it up to you," he said.

"Don't bother," she told him. "I deserved everything I've been through.'' Then she strode away to get the door, while Adam stared after her, brows bent, guts in turmoil. All this time he'd hated her. All this time he'd blamed her. When she'd never had a choice.

And he whispered, ''You're wrong, Kirsten. *Nobody* deserves what you've been through.''

Kirsten pulled the door open. Garrett looked from one of them to the other. His hair was rumpled, as if he'd been pushing his hands through it. ''What took you so long?''

''It's a big house,'' Adam said, but his tone said more. *Leave it alone, big brother.*

Garrett frowned hard, and his eyes went curious, but he left it alone. It was pretty obvious that there were more important things on his mind right now.

''You'd better sit down,'' he told Kirsten, then glanced at Adam. ''You'd *both* better sit down.''

Adam swore. Kirsten rocked back just slightly. So slightly Garrett might not have noticed, but Adam did. He'd been watching her so closely, searching for some sign of what secrets she harbored in the dark places of her heart, that he noticed if she so much as breathed oddly. He took her arm and drew her into the sitting room, a far cozier place than any other room in the house. All wood. Knotty pine. With a fireplace and big, soft furniture that hugged you when you sat down. Adam had discovered the room on his search for Kirsten last night.

Garrett blinked when he stepped into the room. ''This is different.''

''That's because I tore it apart and started over. I

was going to do the whole place, one room at a time, but once Joseph saw what I'd done in here, he forbade me to touch anything else." Kirsten shrugged. "His loss." Her hands fisted together in front of her, and her knuckles were white. "So do we discuss the weather next or get on with the bad news, Garrett?"

Garrett licked his lips and nodded at the sofa, and Kirsten moved toward it but didn't sit down. Adam stayed where he was. "They know about the will, don't they?" he asked, unable to wait for his brother to spill the news.

Garrett's brows went up. "They know *what* about the will?"

Kirsten groaned. Adam sighed and kicked himself. "I'm sorry," he told her.

She shook her head. "He'd have found out sooner or later, anyway." And she glanced at Garrett. "Joseph left me—"

"Don't." Garrett held up both hands. "Kirsten, don't say another word. I swore an oath when I pinned on this badge, and I can't break it. Anything you tell me, I'm gonna be obliged to pass along. And if there's something about that will they don't know yet, well, they'll find out when they find out. The longer it takes them, the better the chance of us finding the real culprit. Understand?"

Blinking, Kirsten nodded.

"What did you come here to tell us, if not about the will?" Adam asked.

"The gun." Garrett worked the brim of his hat between his thumbs and forefingers, turning it in a slow circle in front of him. "The gun was registered to you, Kirsten. Bought a week ago in El Paso by a woman matching your description, carrying your ID."

Kirsten sat down hard, as if some big gust of wind had knocked her off her feet. "No."

"We already know your prints are on it. You admitted you fired the weapon. You were found standing over the body with it. There were no signs of forced entry, nothing stolen...."

"I didn't buy any gun. Garrett, I swear to you, I didn't buy any gun."

"I believe you."

Kirsten lifted her head slowly, met Garrett's eyes. "Do you?"

Garrett nodded, and Adam sighed in relief. She didn't need people doubting her right now.

"Joseph did this," she whispered. "Somehow he paid someone off to go in there and buy that gun, using some kind of identification with my name on it. He must have."

"But why would he want to?" Garrett asked. "Kirsten, you can't seriously think the man planned his own murder...."

Kirsten lowered her head, closed herself down the second the doubt crept into Garrett's voice. "It doesn't matter what I think. I can't prove it. They're going to arrest me, aren't they, Garrett?" Very slowly she looked up.

Garrett nodded. "Later today, I imagine. And if what's in that will is what I'm thinking it is now…maybe sooner. If they can get Hawkins to hand it over. So far he hasn't.''

"We can't just stand by and let this happen.'' Adam paced to where Kirsten sat looking stunned, and he leaned down and pressed his hands to her shoulders. "We're *not* going to let this happen, Kirsty.''

"I don't really see that we can prevent it,'' Garrett said, his voice soft and full of regret.

Shock rippled through Adam like ice water. He straightened and turned to face his brother. "What the hell do you mean, we can't prevent it? She's innocent.''

Garrett shook his head slowly. "Maybe if she had admitted the gun was hers…but she didn't, and that makes it look even—''

"But it *wasn't* mine!''

"I know…I'm just telling you the way it's going to look to everyone else,'' Garrett said.

Kirsten was on her feet again, and tears—not of fear, but of anger—welled in her eyes. Fists clenched at her sides, jaw tight, she paced. "He's doing all of this to me somehow. My God, he's going to make sure I go down with him.''

Garrett met Adam's eyes. "No jury's gonna believe the man would set up his own murder. It's not as if he faked his death and skipped the country, Kirsten. He's in the county morgue, for God's sake.''

"I don't give a damn if he's in the freaking White House,'' Adam said. "Kirsten didn't kill him. And she's not going to jail.''

Garrett looked tortured. "It doesn't mean anything,

Adam. It'll only be temporary. Kirsten, we'll find the truth. You won't be there long. I'll talk to the judge, get him to set bail. We'll get you through this.''

With a sniffle, Kirsten nodded.

"She's *not going to jail*," Adam said again. "Not for one night."

Kirsten touched his shoulder. "Adam, I—"

"No. You've already served two years' hard time. No more." He stepped closer to Garrett, met his brother's eyes. "No more."

"Adam, don't do this." It was a plea.

"Then leave."

"You know I can't. You're gonna run the minute I'm out of sight. Dammit, Adam, I can't just turn around and let you do that."

"You can't stop me, either."

Kirsten stepped between them. "Stop this…Adam, stop—"

Adam pushed her gently aside. "I'm asking you once more. Go home, Garrett."

Garrett shook his head, his eyes sad, sorry, but stubborn all the same. "You'll wind up in jail, too, if you do this. No, Adam, you're gonna sit here and wait for the rangers. We'll do this by the book or—"

Adam hit him. He hit him with everything he had, and he figured the blow probably hurt him as much as it hurt his brother. Garrett's head snapped backward, and he went down like a felled redwood, breaking a coffee table in two on the way.

"Add assaulting an officer to the list of charges,"

Adam said, and he grabbed Kirsten's hand and drew her out of the room.

"Oh, God!" she cried. "Garrett?" She pulled against Adam's grip, turning to try to see if his brother was all right, but Adam kept his hold as he dragged her through the house and out the front door. He didn't think Garrett would follow, but he couldn't be too careful. He paused at his brother's pickup, leaned in and snatched the keys. Then he pressed Kirsten into his own car and got behind the wheel. The Jag roared. The tires spun, then caught, and the car shot forward.

Adam's throat was as dry as sand and so tight no sound emerged when he tried to whisper, "Damn, why did you make me hit you? I'm sorry, Garrett."

Add yet one more crime to the list of unforgivable acts she'd committed against the Brand family, Kirsten thought miserably. She had now managed to turn brother against brother. And there had never been any brothers less likely to turn on one another than the Brands. Never. She'd done the impossible.

And now here they were, she and Adam, skulking around in a dim, dusty stable and actively tempting the wrath of another Brand brother. The one with the hottest temper of all.

"Adam, you've lost your mind!" It was a harsh whisper in the darkness. "Why don't you just let me go? I'll just go off on my own. You can't do this...."

"Will you hush?" Adam whispered back. "If Wes sees us sneaking around his stables, he's liable to shoot first and recognize me as blood kin later. You know his temper. Just trust me, okay?''

She *did* know about Wes Brand's temper. It wasn't something she would like to have directed her way. Yet here she was, trespassing in the stables of his Sky Dancer Ranch, about to steal a pair of the finest Appaloosas in this part of Texas.

''Do they still hang horse thieves?'' she whispered. Adam was opening a stall door, stroking a spotted muzzle and leading a mare out onto the barn floor. One of the few who wasn't expecting a foal. Most of them were, Adam had told her.

''We're only borrowing them.'' He closed the stall door. ''This is Mystic. Hold her halter, Kirsty.''

She did. Adam immediately opened another stall with the name Layla painted on the door and abducted another horse. Kirsten led her own captive closer to a window, so she could watch for Wes and his wife, Taylor, to return home from wherever they'd gone. Or for a shotgun barrel to pop out a window. Neither happened.

Adam stood near the open tack room door now, saddling one mare, then the other. Slipping bridles into place. ''Borrowing'' some saddlebags. He scooped grain into one of them, and that let Kirsten know he was planning on being gone awhile. And that he intended to take good care of his ill gotten transportation.

Then he ripped the tag off the burlap feed bag, flipped it over and wrote a note to his brother on the blank white reverse. She leaned over to see what he could possibly write to explain his actions.

Wes,
If anyone can understand, it ought to be you. I'll take good care of them.
Adam

Kirsten read it, then sighed. "I'd forgotten all about your brother's time in prison," she said.

"For a crime he didn't commit." Adam rolled the note up and stuck it in the wire mesh on the front of one of the empty stalls. "He's not gonna want to see anyone else go through that. I'm betting he won't even tell Garrett the horses are gone."

"Are you sure about that?"

Adam shrugged. "Doesn't matter. Garrett wouldn't look very hard for us even if he did."

"Oh, he wouldn't? You're talking about the same Garrett you just punched out and left lying on my floor back there, right?"

A pained look crossed Adam's face. He covered it quickly. "Right."

Kirsten swallowed the lump in her throat. "Put Layla back in her stall, Adam. I'll leave this one off someplace safe. But I'm going alone."

"The hell you are." The intensity was back, burning in his eyes. And she knew what it meant. She'd known for some time. He still cared for her, the idiot. It had been so much easier, so much safer, when he'd still hated her for what she'd done to him. When had it changed?

"Adam, I've ruined your life twice. I don't intend to do it a third time."

"What do you mean, twice?"

She closed her eyes and didn't answer him right away. "You hit your own brother. Because of me, Adam. You think I don't know how much it hurt you to do that? You think I don't know how close you guys are? 'Mess with one Brand, you mess with them all.' That's what they say about your family around here. Everyone knows how much love…" Her voice broke. Tears choked her, burned in her throat, because she was thinking about the love in that family—the loving parents who'd generated all of it. And how she'd snuffed that love out. "I'm not coming between you and your family. Not again." She bit her lip. "As a matter of fact, I'm not even borrowing your brother's horse."

She spun on her heel and ran out the barn's open rear door. The grassy meadow beyond cushioned every footfall as she ran away. Her feet pounded across the barnyard and into the pasture beyond. She raced toward the trees at its edge, pouring all her anger and frustration and fear into every step. She would head for the border. She would send for her father when it was safe. She would…

Heavy steps came from behind, and then a pair of arms snaked around her and drew her to a clumsy halt. Adam turned her in his arms until she faced him. She was breathless, hot with exertion. So was he. His face flushed with dark color. His eyes sparkled with something. Adrenaline, probably. They stood among some trees near the edge of Wes's pasture, a hundred yards from the barn, farther from the house. The sun beat down, and the breeze ruffled her hair and cooled her heated skin. Adam's arms stayed put, linked at the small of her back. Then they tightened.

She pressed both hands to his chest. Not hard. Just a little, and he went still.

"Where did you think you were going?"

She lifted both shoulders, lowered her head. "To the same place all the wanted murderers go in the movies. Mexico."

He shook his head. "You gonna live on the run for the rest of your life?"

"I guess so," she said. "If I have to. But *you* are not."

"I wasn't planning to."

"Then..." She sent a questioning glance back toward the barn. For a second she thought she'd heard something. A motor or... But the sound faded so fast she must have imagined it.

"What I was planning," Adam said, "was to hide out somewhere...somewhere close. So we can find out who is setting you up, get the proof we need and clear your name, Kirsten."

"The person who is setting me up is beyond our reach, Adam. He's dead."

"That's impossible."

"Nothing's impossible for that man."

Adam's face went still. "He hurt you," he said,

very softly, as if he didn't want to hear his own words. "Didn't he?"

"He was incapable of making me feel anything, Adam. Including pain."

"But physically—" Fear in his eyes. Fear that she would confirm his darkest suspicions.

"If he had, I *would have* shot him."

"If he were still alive, *I* would," Adam said.

She lifted her face, searching his. "Don't do this, Adam. Don't care about me. I ruin everything I touch, and I don't want to ruin you."

He averted his eyes quickly. "I can't stop thinking how things might have been...."

"I wasted years doing that. Believe me, it doesn't help anything."

"But if there could still be a chance..." He looked at her again, dead on target with his piercing sapphire eyes. "Could there...still be a chance for us?"

It was Kirsten's turn to look away. Because tears of regret brimmed in her eyes, tears she didn't want him to see. "No. I'm sorry, but...but no."

She heard his slow sigh. His arms were still anchored around her waist, her hands still resting flat on his chest. She felt his heart pounding against her palm.

"Because I took off. Because I believed the worst all too readily and left when you needed me most," he said. "I ruined any chance we had when I walked away from you, didn't I?"

"No, Adam. I ruined it, not you."

"I didn't love you enough. Hell, I was scared to death you'd do just what you did. Expecting it so damned much that I wasn't even surprised when you didn't show for the wedding. I don't even know why.''

Kirsten did. He'd never given all his heart to her, and she knew *exactly* why. He was afraid to risk it, afraid to love someone utterly and completely and have her vanish from his life one sunny afternoon the way his parents had done. He'd been afraid of love ever since that accident. And *that* was Kirsten's fault, as well.

''You didn't ruin anything, Adam,'' she told him again.

He lifted both hands, releasing her waist, only to frame her face. ''If I didn't…then there's a chance. You still feel something for me, Kirsty, I know you do.''

She had to put a stop to this. It would only hurt him more when he finally knew the whole truth. ''No,'' she said, slamming her eyes closed against the invasion of his. ''I don't.''

''Don't you?'' He was quiet, his breath on her face. ''Open your eyes, Kirsty.''

She did, and stared up into his. Then watched as he moved closer, and his hands slid around to the back of her head, cupping it, tilting it. His lips brushed lightly over hers, his eyes keeping her gaze captive. And then finally they fell closed, and he kissed her. His warm, moist mouth covered hers. His lips moved against hers. His body pressed against hers. The shaking began in her knees and moved up until it encompassed her entire body. She'd shut desire down a long time ago. Now it was alive and screaming again for the only man she'd ever made love with. The only man she'd ever wanted. Her first. God, she wished he could be her last, as well. He could erase everything that had happened in between.

Her arms twined around his neck, and she parted her lips. He tasted good. So good and sweet and familiar. She didn't want to stop. Feeding him from her lips, drinking from his, absorbing his body heat along with his breath. She didn't *ever* want to stop.

A soft nicker made its way to her senses. She ignored it, lost in feeling. She'd dreamed of being in these arms again. So tight around her, strong but tender. The way they'd always been. She kept kissing him, her fingers creeping up into his hair.

Adam lifted his head, dragged in a ragged breath. Kirsten opened her eyes and saw the color in his face and the fire in his eyes. He wanted her.

The nicker came again. This time she looked toward it, maybe because she needed to look away from Adam's eyes and the heat and intensity she saw in them.

One of the horses stood just behind Adam. It tapped a forefoot on the ground and blew its impatience.

"What…how did she…?"

Frowning, Adam turned. The second horse stood only a few yards behind the first. Adam looked beyond them and shook his head. "Wes," he said.

"What?"

"Look. The barn door's closed. I didn't do that." Then he glanced at the matched pair of spotted horses again. "And those saddlebags are bulging now."

They moved forward, Adam speaking softly to the horses, stroking them, before moving around to open a bag and paw through it. "Blankets, matches. A change of clothes for each of us."

Kirsten was busy looking through one of the bags on the other horse. "Food, coffee, tin cups..."

"There's a note," Adam said.

Kirsten turned to watch him pull the rolled bit of paper from the thong that held it in place.

Then he read aloud. "'Midnight. Thompson Gorge. I'll be alone. Elliot.'" Adam's brows met, then rose high. *"Elliot?"*

"I don't...what was Elliot doing here?" Kirsten glanced back toward the barn in search of Adam's youngest brother, but saw no one.

"Must have come by to check on the mares for Wes." Adam shook his head. "He's been doing that once in a while the past couple of weeks. Several are due to foal, and if Wes and Taylor both have to be out for the day, Elliot pops in to make sure the mares are okay." He shook his head. "Damn kid," he muttered.

Kirsten sent him a look. "Your brother's almost twenty-five, Adam. He's hardly a kid."

"He'll always be a kid."

She shrugged. "Well, for a kid, he sure is trying to look out for his older brother, isn't he?" she asked with a nod toward the supplies.

"Yeah, and now he's going to go sticking his nose into a mess of trouble."

Kirsten gripped the pommel and pulled herself into the saddle. "Just like his older brother."

He glanced at her, shook his head, then mounted his own horse. "If he thinks I'm going to show up for this midnight rendezvous, he's nuts."

"What if he knows something, Adam? What if he's coming to warn us about something?"

Adam nudged the horse forward, and Kirsten's fell into step close beside it. Adam sighed, deep in thought, but didn't answer.

They rode across the meadows, and when they reached a gate in the fence, Adam climbed down and opened it, waited while she rode through, then closed it again before mounting up. She had no idea where they were heading. Away. Just away, she thought. And the relief that thought brought with it was like a fresh breeze on a hot day.

"You shouldn't be coming with me," she said after a while.

"I thought we already settled that." They paused near a stream, and the horses bent to drink.

"That kiss back there didn't settle anything. That was just…"

"Just what?" He eyed her sharply.

She gave her head a staccato shake. "Just nerves. Fear. I don't know, just the situation."

He tilted his head very slightly. "You think that's all it was, do you?"

Kirsten nodded. "It didn't mean anything."

"It meant we still want each other, Kirsty. It meant that hasn't changed."

The horses stopped drinking, and they started forward again, picking their way through the thinning grass, stepping carefully over the occasional patch of rocky ground.

"Nothing can happen between us, Adam. Too much has changed. We can never go back."

"You're right," he said. "We can only go forward."

He kicked his horse into a run. Kirsten sat very still for a moment. Adam could be as stubborn as a rusted bolt when he got his mind made up about something. But she had to stop this thing in its tracks. She had to make it clear to him, once and for all. She couldn't let him fall for her again, only to smash his heart to dust when she told him the truth.

So why not just tell him now? Wouldn't that make everything easier? He'd hate you, probably turn and walk away, and you wouldn't have to worry about hurting him later. So why not just tell him the truth and let the poor man go?

She knew why. Even though she hated like hell to admit it, she knew damned well why. Tonight they would be alone together, in hiding, in whatever place he planned to take them. Tonight they would be alone, and maybe he would try to make love to her.

And maybe she wanted him to.

Chapter 7

Adam was going to get to the truth. Because it was killing him not to know. Dammit, he'd spent all this time hating her, blaming her, and now he was busy hating and blaming himself. If he'd done what it was looking more and more as if he had—walked out on the woman he'd claimed to love just when she'd needed him most—damn, how was he supposed to live with that? If he'd stayed, if he'd held on to his temper and confronted her then and there, could he have prevented everything that had happened to her since? The two years of hell that bastard Cowan had apparently put her through? The marriage that never should have been?

My God, had she really been forced into it?

And if so, then how?

Adam was going to get the answers. He'd damned

well been patient long enough. And maybe he'd wronged her, and maybe he'd been a little too ready to believe the worst, but Kirsten *owed* him. Kirsten Armstrong Cowan was going to tell him the truth. She had to.

Not knowing was eating him alive.

He took her to the only place he could think of where she would be safe. Away from town, away from civilization, from comfort and manners and pretense...away from makeup and hair spray and clothes that had become her fortress. He took her into the barren, rocky hell the locals called "the Badlands." A place where there was nothing but jagged rock and hard-packed, desert-dry earth, and raw, brutal honesty.

He was careful, guiding his horse over grit and stone. There might be one person he could think of who would be capable of tracking them, as little sign as they'd left in their wake. But his baby sister, Jessi, was on vacation with her family.

They picked their way deeper into the wilderness, until Adam chose a spot. A high, level bluff with enough boulders for cover and a good view of anyone coming up on them from any direction. Not all that far from Thompson Gorge, either, just in case he decided to meet Elliot there tonight.

He still hadn't made up his mind about that.

"We'll camp here," he said, drawing his mount to a halt, getting off, beginning to undo the straps holding the saddlebags in place. "There's a patch of grass over here for the horses, and a small water hole just down beyond those rocks."

He slid the weighty bags off, set them on a flat-topped boulder and began undoing the cinch. Then he glanced up, because Kirsten was still sitting astride her horse. She frowned at him, the sun slanting on her face and a breeze lifting her hair.

"I still think it would be best to ride for the border."

Adam swallowed his instinctive urge to tell her that she was wrong. She wouldn't react well to being told she was wrong. She never had.

"Look, it's your life. Your decision." He let go of the straps. "If you want me to help you make it to Mexico, I will."

"You will." She repeated it flatly.

"You know I will." He met her eyes, held them for a brief moment, then looked away. "But I'd ask you to give my way a chance first. If it looks like it's not gonna work, we're outta here."

She sat still, just looking down at him. Then Mystic tossed her mane and danced impatiently, but Kirsten moved with the animal without even thinking about it. Never swayed. She'd always been great with horses.

"So you have some kind of a plan, then," she said, eyes narrow. "I should have known. You always have a plan."

"Yeah, well, you caught me on an off day this time, Kirsten. I don't have a clue. Just a vague notion that we could probably hide out by day and do some snooping around by night. See if we can turn up some evidence as to who really did this and why they're setting you up to take the fall."

"We won't find anything."

"Not if we don't try, we won't."

Kirsten sighed. Adam watched the rise and fall of her chest. The play of light on her hair and its flash in her eyes. Something knotted in his gut. His hands clenched at his sides, maybe because it was the only way to keep them there. Okay, so he wasn't over her after all. He'd pretty much shot the theory that he ever had been all to hell. And he knew he was headed for serious trouble here, which was why he had to know the whole story. Why she'd left him. Why she'd married a bastard like Cowan. The whole truth. He needed to know just where he stood with her. Before it was too late. Because he was in danger of getting his heart smashed to bits by Kirsten all over again, and he damned well wasn't planning to let that happen.

"We snoop tonight?" she asked him.

"No. Tonight we lie low. They'll be looking. Tomorrow night we'll slip back into town. They'll all think we're long gone by then."

"And if we don't find anything?"

"Then we try again the next night," he said, watching her face.

"No, we don't. We head to Mexico. Or one of us does, anyway. The other one goes home and says whatever he has to to keep his butt out of jail."

Adam sighed. "It's going to be tough to make any progress in just one night, Kirsty."

"It's that or nothing, Adam. I've got no reason to hang around waiting for someone to slap a life sentence on me. Or worse."

"I'm not going to let that happen. And you've got every reason to hang around."

"You can't stop it from happening. And you're wrong. I'd be long gone by now if not for..." She didn't finish. She didn't have to.

If not for you, that was what she'd been about to say. No reason to hang around, huh? Well, maybe those words would have been more convincing if she hadn't still been here. Even now, getting down off her horse and removing its saddle and blanket.

Adam nodded, satisfied she must have some reason to hang around or she would be riding hard due south right now. He let the horses locate the grass on their own, then gathered up some dry wood for a fire. He was pretty sure he was the reason. He probably shouldn't be thinking that way. But he *liked* thinking that way, dammit. And after the way she'd responded to his kiss back there...

He went still, remembering, tasting those lips and wanting to do it all over again.

"You think that's a good idea?" she asked.

"It's probably a terrible idea," he said. Then he saw her frowning at him and at the fire he was about to light. She was hunkered nearby, unpacking the saddlebags, taking inventory, but she'd paused to stare at him. "Oh, you mean the fire?"

She nodded.

"It's not dark yet. No one will spot the flames if we keep it small. And wood this seasoned isn't gonna make much smoke. We'll need to douse it before dark, though."

"Makes sense. You're not bad at this stuff, for a city boy."

"I've never, *ever* been a city boy, hon."

"Not even when you were there?"

"Nope." He hunkered beside the fire he'd laid, stuck a match to some tinder and watched it flare up. "To tell you the truth, I hated it."

"Then why did you stay?" She sat on a rolled-up blanket to watch the fire take hold.

Adam looked at her. "I told the family it was a great career opportunity. That I loved the big money, the fast life."

One side of her mouth pulled into a small, brief smile. "They believe you?"

"Nah. They said it was 'cause I couldn't stand to be in the same town with you and Cowan." Adam caught her eyes with his and held them fast. "I never admitted it, but they were right."

She rose fast, paced away uneasily, didn't look at him. He stayed where he was, poking the burgeoning fire with a stick, watching her, waiting for a reply.

"I'm going to take the horses down to that watering hole for a drink," she said, and she hurried away.

Avoiding the subject. Well, hell, Adam thought, she couldn't keep it up all night. Sooner or later she would talk to him. He wasn't going to take no for an answer.

Not this time.

Kirsten sat on the ground and watched the horses drink. Adam hadn't followed. She'd half expected him to. He had a determined, stubborn look in his eyes tonight, and she didn't like it. She knew that look. He could be so damned persistent when he made up his mind about something.

She closed her eyes, sat and rehearsed in her mind the words she would say. The way she would tell him. The truth she had to speak. Had to. Because she'd figured something out back there at Sky Dancer Ranch when they'd "borrowed" the horses. When Adam had kissed her. She'd suspected it before, but now she was certain. He still cared. Maybe he'd never stopped. And while his love for her had never been the soul-shattering, gut-wrenching kind she'd felt for him, it had been real. And, fool that he was, he still felt it. He deserved the truth. He deserved to hate her for what she'd done. He deserved to be let off the hook.

Oh, but what might have happened between them tonight if she didn't have to confess?

Tears burned. She blinked at them, but they pooled anyway. Damn Adam for being so beautiful, and so strong, and so...so *Adam.*

"Kirsty?"

Sniffling, she lifted her head, wiped her eyes. He stood behind her. She didn't turn to face him.

"You've been out here awhile. The horses came back without you."

Licking dry lips, she glanced at the water hole where the animals had been, then at the sun resting low on the horizon, halfway to setting already. "I was...thinking."

"Yeah. A lot on your mind, I imagine."

"Yeah."

"Think you can eat? You haven't had a damned thing since breakfast."

A tight smile tugged at her lips. It was just like him to keep track of what she was eating, and how often. To worry. To care. "I could probably manage a few bites. What have you got? Hardtack and beans?" Another brush at her eyes with the heels of her hands. The tears didn't show anymore. Did they?

She looked at him. The smile pulled his lips tight, but it didn't reach his eyes. He stood with his hands in his pockets, looking down at her, hat cocked back on his head. Sun painting his face bronze and gleaming in his eyes.

"You okay?" he asked.

"Sure I am. I'm tougher than I look, you know."

"Yeah. Well…" He sounded doubtful but didn't elaborate. Instead, he held out a hand. She took it and let Adam pull her to her feet. Then she went still, because he held on, his eyes probing hers. "There didn't used to be so many secrets in those brown eyes of yours, Kirsten. They used to sparkle. Now they're dull with worry and…I don't know. Pain."

"Chalk it up to looking down the business end of a murder charge, Adam."

"That's all?"

"Isn't that enough?"

He pursed his lips. Said nothing.

"I smell coffee."

With a sigh and a slight lowering of his chin, he let it go. All of it. His unspoken questions, his suspicions, his need to know. For now. He let it go for the moment, for her, as she'd known he would. Not for anything would he push too hard when he could see pain in her eyes. But she knew him too well to think he wouldn't come back to it later. And keep coming back until he had the answers he wanted. And even if he didn't, she would have to tell him...all of it. And soon.

Adam turned, tucking her hand to his side and heading back toward the fire. "Don't get your hopes up. It's been a while since I've brewed coffee in a tin pot over an open fire."

"Damn. And here I was hoping for cappuccino."

She chose a spot near the fire and sat down. Adam set a small cooler beside her, then used his shirtsleeve as a pot holder and poured coffee into two tin cups. Kirsten opened the cooler and peered inside. Cold fried chicken, a pair of large ice packs, assorted fruit and small covered dishes in varying shapes, sizes and colors were wedged into the thing.

"Elliot tends to be of the belief that so long as there's plenty to eat, all is right with the world," Adam said.

"I remember that about him. And the idea does have merit." She hauled out a golden brown drumstick and bit into it. Flavor exploded in her mouth, and her stomach growled for more.

"He stuffed bread and canned goods into the other pack," Adam said. "Even remembered to include a can opener."

"If I ever see your kid brother again, remind me to thank him."

She took another bite, chewed, swallowed. Reached

for the coffee cup and burned her fingers. When she drew her hand away fast, Adam was there, gripping her hand, turning it.

"It's okay."

"Let me see," he insisted, when she would have pulled away. He examined her hand by the fading blaze of the orange sunset, ran his fingertips over hers. Electric contact. It burned more than the hot tin had.

Kirsten closed her eyes. She wanted him. Damn, how she wanted him.

Satisfied she was okay, he brought her fingers to his lips, kissed them softly.

She drew her hand away so fast she hurt her wrist. "Why did you do that?"

Adam shrugged, but there was fire in his eyes, a spark she knew well. "Old habits...you know." He held her gaze for a long moment, then finally broke eye contact and sighed. He sat down beside her, reaching into the cooler for a piece of chicken. "Sorry. Kissing singed fingers doesn't help much, I imagine. It was something my mother..." He cut himself off there, not finishing the sentence.

Kirsten's stomach turned over. Her appetite fled. "Something...your mother used to do?"

He nodded without looking at her and bit into his chicken.

"You never talked about her. Your mother," she said, very slowly, not even sure why she wanted to torture herself this way. "Not even to me."

He didn't reply. Not until he'd cleaned the meat to the bone and started on a second piece. Then he paused, saw she was still looking at him, awaiting a reply, and shrugged. "Some things...a man just doesn't want to discuss."

"Not even with a woman he claimed to love?"

Adam stilled. "I never *claimed* to love you, Kirsty. It was real, not alleged. Hell, never mind. How did we get on this subject, anyway?"

"I asked you about your mother. How old were you, Adam, when your parents were killed? Sixteen?"

His lips thinned, but he answered. "Fifteen."

"You must have been...crushed."

"That'd be one word for it." He sipped his coffee, looked back toward town, in search, she thought, of another subject. A safer one. But there was an old pain in his eyes. One she had put there.

"I'm sorry," she whispered.

Adam got an odd, squinty look. "Nothing for you to apologize for, Kirsty. It wasn't your fault."

Oh, but it was. "Adam..." She drew a breath, squeezed her hands together. It was time. "Adam, I—"

"I should be the one apologizing," he said.

Kirsten's brows drew together. "What—"

"For never talking about...about that. To you. I mean, it was the worst time of my life, and, hell, let's face it. It changed me. You had a right to know about that. To understand why I was...the way I was."

She had understood. Or she'd thought she had. But he was right, they'd never discussed it. And she wasn't sure she wanted to now. Why the hell had she started this?

"The truth is, it damn near killed me, losing them."

She closed her eyes. Felt his pain. Heard it in his voice and sensed it emanating in waves from his soul.

"I knew the second Garrett came to me that something terrible had happened. I'd never seen that big lug cry before. Never in my life. It scared the hell out of me. He…gathered all of us together in the parlor. Me, Ben, Elliot, Wes…even little Jessi, though she was so damned tiny she didn't really know what was going on. Thank God for that."

Kirsten's mind told her to look away, not into his eyes, into his pain-racked face as he remembered. Change the subject, shut him out.

But her heart cried more loudly. Heal him. Hold him. Make his horrible pain go away. But how could she, when she was the one who'd put it there?

"He made us all hold hands, and then he told us. Mama and Dad wouldn't be coming home to the Texas Brand again. He said they'd gone to heaven, that they were safe with the angels now, and watching over us just the way they always had. But from above."

Her heart broke. It just shattered. He was opening up to her in a way he'd never done before.

"The others cried. All of them. Even Jessi, when she saw her big brothers all reduced to tears like that. But not me. I didn't shed a tear. I got mad," he confessed, lowering his head, sweeping his hat off and holding it between his knees by the brim. "Furious. I kept asking myself how my parents could do something like that, how they could go off to live with the angels while the six of us stayed behind to fend for ourselves.''

Kirsten touched his face. ''It wasn't really anger, Adam. It was pain. You just had to direct it somehow. You were a child.''

''Oh, it was anger. I blamed them. Both of them, for abandoning us. Abandoning me. I vowed then and there that I'd never love anyone that much again. Never give anyone the chance to leave me that way again.''

''It was,'' she whispered, searching for words, ''it was a natural reaction.''

''Maybe. Maybe not. If it was, it should have passed. I should have been able to work through it, do my mourning, make my peace. I didn't, Kirsten. To tell you the truth, I'm still angry.'' He lowered his head, shook it slowly. ''But then you came along.''

She nodded. ''I know. And you wouldn't let yourself fall all the way in love with me. Because you were half convinced I'd leave you the same way they did.''

''I was *fully* convinced you'd leave me the way they did,'' he said very slowly. ''And totally determined not to fall all the way in love with you. I told myself I wouldn't. I even convinced you of it, didn't I?''

Studying his face, she nodded.

Adam looked into her eyes. Lifting one hand to cup her cheek, he let his gaze move from her forehead to her chin and back to her eyes again. ''Fooled everybody, then. Because I *did* fall all the way. I did, Kirsty. And when you walked out on me, I didn't think I'd survive. Wasn't even sure I wanted to.''

She closed her eyes. She'd wanted so badly to hear him speak to her this way, once. A long time ago. But not now. Sweet God, not now.

"And I never really fell out again, either," he went on.

"Don't, Adam—"

"That's my deep dark secret, Kirsty. The one I've been fighting tooth and nail to keep, even from myself. That's it. And I thought it was about time I told you."

Tears streaming down both cheeks now, she opened her eyes and stared through hazy pools at him. "Why, Adam? Why now?"

"Because," he said slowly, "it's only fair. It's your turn now, Kirsten. Tell me the dark secrets you've been keeping. Tell me the truth."

Sniffling, she shook her head. "I...I can't...."

"Yeah, you can," he told her. "'Cause neither one of us is leaving here until you do."

Sitting up straighter, Kirsten drew her knees to her chest, hugged them, stared into the flames. What was she waiting for? Why didn't she just blurt it all out? Her throat hurt. Her head ached. The fire danced. She licked her lips. Where the hell was she supposed to begin? Her voice hoarse, she closed her eyes and forced words through the narrow space in her throat. "What do you want to know?"

Adam sat very still beside her. "Did you ever love me?"

She nodded into her knees without hesitation. "I've never loved anyone else." And even to her own ears, her voice sounded desolate. Utterly without hope.

She didn't look at him. She couldn't. She just listened. The night was slowly coming to life now. A distant bird called. A coyote cried the way her heart was doing—a mourning, warbling, broken sound that said better than words could what her life had become. The fire hissed and snapped.

"Then you never loved Cowan."

"I never even liked him."

"He forced you to marry him," Adam said softly. Leading her by the hand with his words, trying to make it easier for her to get to the truth. "He had something on you, something he held over your head. And you married him to keep him quiet."

Kirsten nodded.

"What was it, Kirsten?"

Silence. She tried to part her lips, to speak, but her jaws seemed to have locked up. He waited a long time. She tried to make herself say the words. *I killed your parents. I orphaned your baby sister and your brothers. I took away your life and changed it forever.*

"Tell me."

"Please, Adam, don't make me do this."

"It's time, Kirsten."

She shook her head hard. "I...I *can't!*"

He was silent for a long moment. Brooding. "Maybe I can help get you started. Whatever he had on you, it had to have been pretty bad." Less patience in his tone now. A hint that maybe he couldn't quite conceive of *anything* that bad. "Bad enough that you were willing to become his wife—not just on paper, but in every way. Willing to lie in his bed."

Her head came up, eyes wide.

"You talk more than you should when you're drunk," he told her. "You talked about him trying to get you pregnant. About him grunting and sweating on top of you night after night…" He closed his eyes as some emotion rushed through them—an emotion that looked to her like disgust.

She felt Adam's anger, understood it. Jealousy. It enraged him to think of her making love to another man. Of course it did. But it enraged *her* to hear him talk to her this way. "I was *never* willing. I had no choice."

"You had a choice!" His temper long gone, he shouted the words, lost now to reason. "The choice was to come to me, Kirsty. To tell me the truth. You think I wouldn't have stopped him? You think I'd have let him make you his—" He bit his lip, slammed his hat to the ground and kicked it viciously.

"His whore?" Kirsten finished softly.

Adam turned, blinking, a little of the rage fading. "No. That's not what I—"

"Why not? That's exactly what I was. His whore. He paid for my services by keeping quiet about what he knew. And I lay there and took it just as often as he demanded it. I lay there, and I felt nothing but revulsion. I thought about running. I thought about suicide. And yes, I thought about murder. But hell, Adam, you know me. You know how stubborn I am. I decided I'd beat him. I'd get something just as damaging on him, and then I'd turn the tables. But it never happened. The only thing that happened was that I let him use me just the way you say I did. Night after night, over and over, I lay in his bed, and the only thought in my mind was that I wished it were you there with me. Your hands on me. Your body… But it wasn't. It wasn't. It never will be again.''

She lowered her fisted hands to her sides, stubbornly refusing to cry anymore. She would not cry anymore.

"I'm sorry."

"Don't be," she said.

He put his hand on her shoulder. She shrugged it off.

"I shouldn't have said… Kirsten, the thought of him touching you…''

"I was paid well. Hell, I inherited everything the bastard owned. Or will if I ever find proof I didn't murder him.''

Adam put a hand to the back of her head, stroked her hair. "You don't want his money. You never wanted it.''

"You don't know a thing about what I want. Hell, Adam, you don't even know what *you* want anymore.''

"Yeah," he said. "Yeah, I do.'' But he took his hand away. As soon as he did, Kirsten got to her feet and walked away from him. And he let her go.

Chapter 8

Great. Couldn't he have waited at least until she'd finished her meal to insult her, alienate her and take his frustration out on her? What the hell kind of idiocy possessed him with Kirsten, anyway? Jealousy, that was part of it. Plain old jealousy, bigger and more powerful than anything he'd ever felt in his life. And anger. Yes, anger at her for not coming to him with all of this two years ago. For not trusting him with the truth. For not letting him fix it for her. And at himself, for walking away. For not seeing the truth behind her lies. For letting her go.

God, he never should have let her go.

She belonged with him. The very thought of Cowan having touched her, much less…

No. He wouldn't think about that now. He'd let his anger come out all wrong, directed it at her when she'd

FREE FREE
BOOKS! GIFT!

PLAY BANGO!

AND CLAIM 2 FREE BOOKS
AND A FREE GIFT!

BANGO

9	19	44	52	71
4	20	32	50	68
11	18	FREE	53	63
7	27	36	60	72
3	28	41	47	64

BANGO

5	19	32	54	73
6	17	41	50	6
13	22	FREE	52	
5	24	44	46	
8	21	35	47	75

★ No Cost!
★ No Obligation to Buy!
★ No Purchase Necessary!

TURN THE PAGE TO PLAY →

PLAY BANGO!

AND GET THREE FREE GIFTS!

It looks like BINGO, it plays like BINGO but it's FREE

HOW TO PLAY:

1. With a coin, scratch the Caller Card to reveal your 5 lucky numbers and see that they match your Bango Card. Then check the claim chart to discover what we have for you — FREE BOOKS and a FREE GIFT. All yours, all free!

2. Send back the Bango card and you'll receive 2 brand-new Silhouette Intimate Moments® novels. These books have a cover price of $4.25 each in the U.S. and $4.75 each in Canada, but they are yours to keep absolutely free.

3. There's no catch. You're under no obligation to buy anything. We charge nothing — ZERO — for your first shipment. And you don't have to make any minimum number of purchases — not even one!

4. The fact is, thousands of readers enjoy receiving books by mail from the Silhouette Reader Service® months before they are available in stores. They like the convenience of home delivery and they love our discount prices!

5. We hope that after receiving your free books you'll want to remain a subscriber. But the choice is yours — to continue or cancel, any time at all! So why not take us up on our invitation, with no risk of any kind. You'll be glad you did!

YOURS FREE!

This exciting mystery gift is yours free when you play BANGO!

If offer card is missing write to: Silhouette Reader Service, 3010 Walden Ave., P.O. Box 1867, Buffalo, NY 14240-1867

BUSINESS REPLY MAIL
FIRST-CLASS MAIL   PERMIT NO. 717   BUFFALO, NY

POSTAGE WILL BE PAID BY ADDRESSEE

SILHOUETTE READER SERVICE
3010 WALDEN AVE
PO BOX 1867
BUFFALO NY 14240-9952

NO POSTAGE
NECESSARY
IF MAILED
IN THE
UNITED STATES

been as much a victim in all of this as anyone. He shouldn't have done that. His anger belonged to a dead man. And that made it all the more frustrating. There was no target now. No use for the fury raging like a cyclone inside him. He had to let it go. *He had to let it go.*

But letting it go was harder than it sounded. Because there was still that other fury swirling around in his heart, feeding this one, empowering it. And that old anger had been around for so long, he wasn't sure he knew how to get rid of it.

Kirsten lay bundled up in a blanket on the ground, all the way on the other side of the fire. She was not sleeping. There was nothing relaxed or restful about her. Still, yes, but taut, rigid. He doubted she would close her eyes all night.

He should have kept his mouth shut. There would be time enough for the truth later. After Cowan's murderer was caught and put behind bars. After Kirsten's name was cleared and things got back to…normal.

Hell, things hadn't been *normal* since his would-be wedding day. He didn't think his life would ever be *normal* again.

And he had blown it with Kirsten tonight. That was for sure. She would never open up to him if he kept putting her on the defensive about Cowan. And they would never have a chance if he couldn't find a way to forgive that…to forget. To put it in the past.

But right now, it was just a little too fresh for that.

With a sigh, Adam gathered up the cooler, tied a cord around it and carried it to the water hole to keep the leftover food relatively cool for the night. Then he picketed the horses near the grass and carefully doused the campfire. He did every job he could think of to do, just to kill the time. To vent his frustration. To ease the tension in his mind and his body. But when he'd finished them all, Kirsten still hadn't moved so much as a muscle, and he was still as tense as a whipcord. He didn't know what to say to her. What to do. How to fix this.

He chose a boulder with a good view of both the surrounding night and of Kirsten, and he sat watch. It was going to be, he thought, a very long night.

He was right. The minutes dragged by like hours, and then became hours that seemed to last for days. His head nodded. He snapped it upright. His eyelids drooped. He pried them open. The moon rose high, lopsided and waxing toward full. Big and yellow. Lonely. Cold. It got damned cold out here at night. Cacti dotted the splitting desert ground, standing like bandits caught by the law. Hands up. No colors out here at night. Shades of gray. No black and white. Was there a message hidden in there somewhere for him?

Soft footsteps made him swing his head around. Kirsten stood behind him, her blanket wrapped around her shoulders. A tin cup in her hand. She handed it to him. He just looked at it.

"Coffee," she said. "It's still slightly warm. I thought you could use a cup."

"Thanks." He took a drink, grimaced at the taste, but drank some more.

"So, are you going to sit up here all night?"

"Thought I might."

She went silent, turned and leaned her back against the rock. He sat atop the same hunk of stone, so she was close to his legs. Not close enough.

Should he apologize again? Try to explain how the image of a woman who should have been his wife in the bed of another man could make a man crazy? Cause him to say mean, hurtful things? He only knew Joe Cowan was one lucky son of a gun to be dead right now. 'Cause if he were alive, Adam would be out for blood. And it would be slow. The bastard had forced Kirsten...he'd forced her. God, Adam wanted to make that reality go away.

He looked at her. Moonlight gleamed in her round wounded eyes. No makeup now. She wore the jeans and T-shirt she'd found in the saddlebag, and her hair hung down long and loose. She looked like the girl he'd fallen in love with. And the years almost seemed to fall away.

"Kirsty, I, uh..."

"You ought to go meet with your brother," she said, interrupting him.

"What?" His brothers were the last thing on Adam's mind right now.

"Elliot. He said in his note to meet him at Thompson Gorge at midnight. I think you should go."

"Why?"

She tipped her head back to look up at him. "Because he might have some kind of information for us. Maybe he's learned something—"

"He doesn't know anything," Adam assured her.

She tilted her head. "You won't know that unless you meet him." Adam pursed his lips. "I know you don't want to drag him into my mess, Adam," Kirsten rushed on. "But he's already involved. He knows we're out here, he gave us supplies, and maybe he's even been digging around on his own."

"Damn fool kid's liable to get himself killed. At least get brought up on charges."

Her brows creased. "You underestimate him, you know. He's not a kid anymore." Crossing her arms over her chest, she added, "And I don't want him getting into trouble because of me any more than you do. So don't you think we ought to see what he's been up to? Find out just what he's doing and tell him to stay out of it?"

With a sigh, he nodded. "I suppose you're right."

"Then let's go. It's eleven-thirty now." She straightened away from the boulder.

Adam slid to the ground, caught her shoulders in his hands and turned her around.

"What?"

"Two things." He pulled his lips tight. "Maybe three."

"Well?"

"One...I shouldn't have said the crap I did before. I didn't mean it. It was foolish male pride and jealousy, and I know damn good and well you've never been any man's whore. I'm sorry. I mean it."

Licking her lips, she lowered her head.

"Two...I want you to stay behind while I go to see Elliot."

"No way in—"

"Suppose he was followed?"

"He's smarter than that," she argued.

"Maybe, and maybe not. The point is, why risk it? If someone's watching him and they see you, all three of us are going to wind up in one of Garrett's cells. So I want you to stay here."

She made a face, lifted her head, but didn't argue. "And three?" she prodded.

"Three?" Adam looked down at her. The round dark wells of her eyes. Hair loose now, and tumbling. The spray had worn off hours ago, so her artificial curls had given way to the natural waves. His voice went coarse and gravelly. "Oh, yeah. Three." He bent down and touched her lips with his, kissed her gently, slowly, as tenderly as he could manage. Tasting her upper lip, her lower one, softly tracing their shape with his tongue. He felt her tremble, heard her catch her breath. Then he lifted his head away. "Three is just this. I still love you. And I want you back."

Every part of her went hard. Stiff. Her eyes seemed rounder and wider than he'd ever seen them.

"When I make love to you again, Kirsty, I'll make you forget Cowan ever touched you. I'll burn that memory away. I'll make it better, I swear it."

Shaking her head hard from side to side, she backed away. "No. You don't know what you're saying."

"Yeah," he said. "I do. And I'm not gonna give up. I'm here for you, Kirsty, and no matter what you do, I'm not gonna give up on you this time. I'm not gonna go running off to lick my wounded pride. If I hadn't done that before, you wouldn't be in this mess now. I might be stubborn, but I'm not stupid. I learn from my mistakes.''

For a long moment she was quiet. Adam decided he'd rendered her speechless. He was pretty surprised by his declarations himself. Enough said. He grabbed his hat off the boulder behind him and dropped it on his head. ''Guess I'll go meet Elliot now.''

''Adam, wait.''

He paused, turned around.

''I want there to be no mistake about this,'' she said slowly. ''The trouble I'm in is no one's fault but my own. Do you understand? No one's. I brought this on myself, and I probably deserve every bit of it. Whatever the outcome. Remember that.''

''No, you don't—''

''Yes, I do. You don't know all the things I've done, Adam.''

''But I will. Just as soon as you tell me.'' He cupped her cheek. ''When I get back, okay? We'll talk when I get back.''

She lowered her head, nodded once. Later, Adam thought he should have seen the warning in her eyes, just before she looked away from his. He should have seen it.

But he didn't.

He just let go of her and headed back to where he'd picketed the horses. Saddled Layla and rode away, off to Thompson Gorge, where it was said the ground was soaked with century-old blood and the spirits of the dead still lingered on nights like tonight.

The way he shivered as the Appaloosa's hooves plodded slowly into the box canyon, Adam could believe it was true.

He looked ahead, left and then right. Saw nothing but the tall, jagged stone walls. The barren ground, dry and splitting. The ghostlike movement of a tumbleweed rolling in slow motion across the unforgiving earth. The occasional dust devil swirling like a living thing in the moonlight.

And then other hoofbeats sounded. Soft. Slow. Coming closer. A rider emerged from the darkness, a gun held in his hand.

Kirsten was already dressed for the journey. Not in the clothes of Mrs. Joseph Cowan, but in a pair of borrowed jeans and a T-shirt, with a denim shirt from the saddlebags for added warmth. Her uniform was gone. Her pretend face. Her make-believe self. Gone, leaving her stripped bare, at the mercy of the elements. There would be no more hiding. No more rich-man's-wife routine, no more attitude. She was just Kirsten Armstrong. She was just a liar and a murderer on the run from the law. No makeup kit or closet full of clothing was going to change that. Not even the love of a man like Adam Brand could change that.

It was no good. No good staying here with Adam and watching him fall for her all over again. No good feeling those old feelings for him trying to pry their way out of the prison where she'd kept them locked away all this time. None of that was any good at all.

She crammed some of the supplies into one set of

saddlebags; then she saddled the remaining horse and mounted up. This was her fight. Not Adam's. She'd dragged herself into this mess alone, and she would damned well get out of it alone. She'd ruined enough lives.

She turned Mystic around and started for the border. She would have plenty of time. She figured the canyon where Adam had gone to meet his brother was a half hour's ride from here. By the time Adam got there and back, she would have a solid head start. And if he was smart, he wouldn't bother following her, anyway.

She dug in her heels, leaned low over the sleek, muscled neck and held on. The mare sailed through the night like a cloud across the face of the moon. Gloriously chilled air rushed over Kirsten's face, lifted her long hair. Animal heat warmed her where her legs held tight to the horse's sides, and she felt those powerful muscles bunching and lengthening beneath her.

It had been a long time since she'd done anything like this…given anything in her life this kind of rein. Run headlong through the night and let the thrill of it invigorate her to the marrow. The stars glittered down, and the moon lit her way. A silver strand glistened ahead, a stream, and she leaned, squeezed, spoke softly. The mare jumped it easily, landing again and never breaking stride. This was good. And freedom lay just ahead.

Freedom…

She'd thought freedom had come when she'd found her husband lying dead on that cold marble floor. But it hadn't. Joseph still imprisoned her, even from death.

Now she thought she would find this elusive thing—this freedom she craved—on the far side of the Mexican border. But would she?

She eased her seat, let up on the mare. Their pace slowed, and Kirsten asked herself just what it was she wanted freedom *from*. Prison? A murder charge? Yes, certainly those things. But what about Texas? Her home, her town? What about her father? How would she ever fulfill her promise to get him out of the nursing home, to bring him to live with her, if she were a fugitive for the rest of her life? Did she really think she would ever be able to send for him? Take him down there to live with her? How would she explain the false names she would have to use? How would she get him the heart transplant he so desperately needed?

And what about Adam?

''And now we get to the truth, don't we?'' she whispered.

She slowed the horse to a walk, lowered her head. He was what she was really running from. Adam Brand, the man she'd always loved, and the truth she'd kept hidden from him. The horrible secret it was going to kill her to tell. That was why she'd run from him in the first place.

Why she'd kept on running ever since. Why she was still running.

Because the fact was, running away from the truth had been easier than facing Adam with what she'd done. Watching the love in his eyes turn to hatred. Seeing the pain, the hurt. And it was still easier.

She swallowed against the dryness in her throat and looked ahead. Lights here and there, where the border patrol lay in wait. More officers than usual out here tonight. Probably because they had a fugitive to hunt down. Kirsten licked her lips, moved more slowly, strained her eyes to see where the men were, and hunted for a spot between them, where she could slip past unnoticed.

Then one of the lights flashed from someplace far too close, shining right into her eyes. She lifted one hand instinctively to block the glare, and a man's voice yelled, "Hold it right there!"

Jerking the reins hard, Kirsten ducked low, whirled the horse around and kicked her sides. The mare leapt into motion, then picked up speed even more when a gunshot—a frighteningly close gunshot—split the night's silence. And then dozens of others rang out in answer—coming from farther away, but aimed at her, every one of them.

"Adam?" Elliot lowered the gun when he got close enough to confirm it was his brother he'd been pointing it at.

"Put that damn thing away," Adam snapped. "You trying to get yourself killed?"

"Trying to help you out of a mess of trouble, big brother. Not that you seem to be any too grateful."

"I'm not. I don't want you involved in this."

"Too late," Elliot said. He holstered his gun, got off his horse. Adam noticed the lean grace with which he moved, the power he seemed to hold in check. Hell,

Kirsten was right. His kid brother *wasn't* a kid anymore.

Adam dismounted as well, swallowed the scolding tone that kept trying to creep into his words, and instead clasped Elliot's hand. When had it become so big, so callused? "Thanks for the supplies."

"No problem. Where are you staying?"

"Made camp not far from here. For now. We're gonna have to move around a lot."

Elliot nodded. "Garrett didn't sound the alarm. I wanted to make sure you knew that. He tried to stall, never said a word about whatever the hell happened at the estate this morning. The rangers never knew you and Kirsten were missing until they showed up to place her under arrest." Elliot paused, eyeing his brother. When Adam didn't speak, he said, "I saw the bruise on Garrett's jaw, Adam. The rest I've been piecing together on my own."

Adam lowered his head, guilt rising like bile in his throat. "He didn't give me any choice."

"The hell he didn't. He's our brother, Adam. He wouldn't have—"

"He was going to let them arrest her."

"Well what the hell did you expect him to do? He's the sheriff, and she's wanted for murder."

Adam shrugged, shook his head. "Is Garrett okay?"

Elliot just stared at him. Then his smile finally came back. Slowly, but surely. "What? You afraid you hurt him?" Elliot's grin grew wider. "You are, aren't you? You sure do have an active fantasy life, pardner. Garrett's got fifty pounds on you. You might be better asking yourself why big brother Garrett went down so easy, instead of wondering how bad you might have hurt him. If he had hit you back, you'd be in a coma right now."

Licking his lips, biting back an angry retort based solely on his own ego, Adam paused, thought back and finally sighed. "You're right. He did go down awfully easy."

"'Course I'm right." Elliot shrugged. "I mean, not to belittle that bruise on his jaw or anything—you always did have a solid right hook—but this is Garrett we're talking about here."

Adam's guilt grew even bigger. "He let us go," he said slowly.

"Damn straight he did. Then, when the rangers came out later in the day and found you two gone, they accused Garrett of aiding and abetting. Threatened to bring him up on charges, but I think he managed to convince them he was completely unaware you'd left. And now they've got a full-fledged manhunt going on."

"I figured as much." Adam lowered his head, sighed. "Listen, all I want to do is buy some time. Find out who killed that bastard, pin a medal on him, and then see to it Kirsten doesn't end up doing his time for him."

Elliot sighed, too, hunkered down. "I kinda figured that was the plan. But how are you gonna do any digging when you can't get back into town?"

"I'll think of something."

"I could—"

"No."

"But if I—"

"Absolutely not."

"Adam, for crying out—"

"No, Elliot."

Elliot's jaw went tight. He held his brother's gaze, his own every bit as stubborn. And then he pulled a hand out of a pocket. It had a brown plastic prescription bottle in it. He held it out. Adam took it.

"What is this?" Joseph Cowan's name was on the bottle. And the name of the drug it contained was one that was familiar. "Percodan?" Adam glanced at Elliot for an explanation.

"I found it in the medicine cabinet in Cowan's master bathroom when I...er...broke into the house today."

"You broke into the—"

"I thought you ought to know about it."

Adam sighed, turned in a circle and pushed his hat off his head. When he faced Elliot again, he shook his head. "The rangers left this?"

Elliot shrugged. "Probably didn't see anything too strange about a pill bottle in a medicine cabinet. Maybe they didn't recognize it for what it was. I wouldn't have myself, except for Doc prescribing it for me when I was seventeen and got thrown by the bull—"

"Thrown and then stomped by the prize bull you'd decided you could ride," Adam said. "I remember. You were broken in so many places, the whole family ached."

"But, Adam, why the hell would Cowan have been taking a painkiller this powerful? This stuff is a narcotic, for crying out loud."

Adam blew a sigh. "You got me. It's a damned good question. But, Elliot, I don't see what this could have to do with the murder. He didn't die from any drug overdose. It was a bullet in the middle of his forehead that put the bastard in hell where he belongs."

"I don't know. I don't know. Maybe nothing. But it's all I could come up with."

Adam stared at the label, willing the bottle to talk to him.

"You've still got it bad for Kirsten, don't you, Adam?"

Looking up sharply, Adam saw the knowledge in his brother's eyes...the brother who was no kid anymore. Finally he just lowered his head again.

"Hell, we all saw it from the minute you came back here. You were the only one who didn't."

"Yeah, well, she's keeping a whole pile of secrets, Elliot. And I don't know if she's gonna be ready to trust any man again any time soon."

"Shoot, you're not any man. You're my brother."

He felt his lips pull into a half smile. "Thanks, Elliot. That means a lot."

Elliot smiled back, slapped Adam's shoulder and turned toward his horse. And that was when the echo of distant gunfire came floating on the breeze, ringing and bouncing off the canyon walls, making it impossible to judge direction or how many shots or anything else.

But Adam's heart froze over, and that was all he needed to know. "Kirsty..." He leapt into the saddle and spurred the horse toward camp, where he'd left her. But he had a sick feeling he wouldn't find her there.

He was halfway there before he realized his kid brother was riding right alongside.

They passed the camp, and he knew without much more than a glance that Kirsten wasn't there. No horse, no sign of life. She'd bugged out on him. Headed for the border. Hell, she was running from him all over again.

They rode hell-bent for leather, and the shooting became louder. The horse blew hard, digging her hooves into the dirt, throwing clumps behind them and thundering over the barren ground. And finally Adam saw her. Kirsten was heading right for them, her horse running like the wind, her body bent over, almost horizontal to the animal's. Beyond her, lights and motion. ATVs and spotlights, bounding over the rugged terrain.

"Take her and go," Elliot shouted. "Go on. I'll stall them."

"Elliot, you can't—"

"Have a little faith in the kid, will you?" Elliot said with a grin, and then he clicked his tongue at his horse, and the two rode off in the direction of the border patrol. Elliot seemed to be setting a course for a direct interception.

Left with little choice, Adam turned his horse around and caught up to Kirsten.

She was breathless. Her face as pale as the moonlight, her eyes wide. She stared at him as he rode up beside her, but she didn't say a word.

"Come on," Adam said. "This way." And he guided her up into the craggy foothills, into cover. It would be tough for anyone to find them here, and he didn't really expect the border guard to try. They had to keep their posts. They could call in reinforcements, of course, but if he knew Elliot, and he did, by now the kid was spinning a yarn that would throw them off the scent.

Within a few minutes, the sounds of pursuit seemed to have stopped. So had the shooting.

"Right here. Come on." Adam slid off his horse on a boulder-strewn hillside and reached up to help Kirsten down, as well. She came. No resistance, no argument, and not a word. Her feet hit the ground. Her knees followed.

"Hey, hey, careful now." Adam closed his arms around her, tugged her upward. The rag doll response was what finally tipped him off. Her head hung on a limp neck, and her hair was in her eyes.

"Kirsten?" He pulled her upright and pushed the hair aside so he could look at her face. But her eyes were closed, and his hand came away wet and sticky. "Kirsty!"

He shook her. No response. Gathering her up, he pushed her hair aside and turned her face toward the moonlight so he could see the damage.

But all he could see was the blood.

Chapter 9

Kirsten's head hurt. She opened her eyes slowly and tried to see through the haze and the pain. It smelled funny here. The surface she lay on…stiff and soft, not the hard-packed ground. A shape came into focus. A face. A dear, familiar face.

"Adam?"

He leaned closer, his hands on her face, smoothing her hair. "It's all right. You're okay. I'm right here, Kirsten, and you're gonna be just fine."

Blinking, she tried to see him clearly, but she couldn't. His face swam and danced in front of her. Her bed tilted, and she felt certain she was about to be dumped onto the floor. She reached for Adam, and he was there, gripping her shoulders, his hands strong and solid. The sensation of falling faded. The room around her straightened, and she relaxed. "Don't let go," she whispered.

"I don't plan to."

When she opened her eyes again, her vision was clearer. Adam stood beside her, one hand still holding her shoulder, the other gently stroking her hair. Around her, the familiar accoutrements that told her she was in a doctor's office. Stainless steel and glass, bottles and bandages. The giant domed light above her. The tall white scales in the corner.

And Adam. Holding her. Holding on to her just the way he'd promised he would.

She remembered then. The wild ride, the gunshots that had followed her, pursuing her like death itself. The burning pain and paralyzing shock of a bullet slamming into her head like a red-hot mallet. The moment of horror as she realized she'd been shot.

Lifting one shaking hand, she touched the spot from which the pain seemed to emanate, and found thick, soft bandages there.

"It was only a graze."

"Was it? It felt more like a freight train," she muttered.

"I'll bet it did. Here, take this." He slipped a tablet between her lips, then cupped her head, lifted her and held a paper cup to her mouth. She sipped the water, swallowed the pill. "Tylenol with codeine," Adam told her, lowering her head to the pillow once more. "It's mild, but it ought to help with the pain."

She nodded, then looked around the oddly silent place for the doctor.

"We're alone," Adam said, reading her the way he always had. "It's only 3:00 a.m. Lucky for us, Doc doesn't have any fancy locks on his office doors. Just a simple tumbler that's easy as hell to pop open."

Holding her throbbing head with one hand, she sat up slowly. "Adam, that's illegal.... God, stealing drugs...you're going to wind up in jail."

"Not unless we get caught."

"Jail's the least of your worries, you two."

Adam's head came up fast, and Kirsten's heart jumped...but settled as she recognized Elliot's voice. The youngest Brand brother came light-stepping his way through the clinic and found them in the little treatment room. Squinting through the darkness, he nodded a greeting toward his brother. Then he came closer to Kirsten, eyeing her with real concern.

"I saw the blood. Figured I'd find you here. I wondered which one of you took the bullet. You okay, Kirsten?"

"It hurts like hell, but Adam says it's just a graze and I'll be fine."

Adam pocketed the pill bottle he'd taken from Doc's locked cabinet. "You sure you weren't followed here?" he asked, and his tone was sharp.

"You think I'm an idiot?" Elliot countered.

Adam only sighed. "What the hell happened out there, El? Since when do the border guys shoot first and ask questions later?"

"Since never." Elliot shifted his worried gaze from Kirsten to Adam and back again. "I talked to them. Convinced them I was just an innocent passerby out for a midnight ride and that I'd unwittingly stumbled into the cross fire. And then I asked them the same damn thing. Why they were firing at shadows in the night.''

''And what was their answer?'' Adam prodded.

''They claim the shadow shot first.''

Both men looked at Kirsten sharply. She blinked, confused. ''I don't understand.''

''The officers swear you shot at them, Kirsten,'' Elliot explained. ''They say they returned fire, but only after you fired at them. And frankly, hon, I'm inclined to believe them.''

She blinked at him, so confused the dizziness returned. ''But...I didn't even have a gun.''

''I know that,'' Elliot said.

''But somebody did,'' Adam said slowly, thinking aloud. ''Somebody fired at those border guards.''

''I don't understand.'' Kirsten searched both men's faces, saw the knowing glance the two brothers exchanged, the nod of affirmation that passed between them. As if they'd already figured out something she wasn't seeing just yet.

''Those boys are too well trained to just start shooting at shadows, Kirsten,'' Adam said, his eyes on his brother. ''I don't think they would have fired if they hadn't believed you did. And I think that's just what someone wanted them to believe. Somebody fired the first shot. But it wasn't you, and it wasn't the border patrol.''

''Whoever it was, they did it deliberately,'' Elliot

added. "Knowing damn well it would force the border patrol to return fire."

"And they damn near got you killed," Adam finished. He stood in front of her, staring into her eyes, his own so tortured that she could feel his pain. "Thank God it didn't work," he whispered. And he pulled her against him, held her. His heat warmed her, and his heart beat hard against her. "Thank God you're okay."

Her arms crept around his waist. She didn't want him to let her go.

"Why did you run away, Kirsty?"

She closed her eyes. "I...I thought it would be better for you if I just...got the hell out of your life, once and for all."

He shook his head slowly, staring down at her. "Honey, you tried that once. It didn't work."

"I know," she whispered. Then, slowly, she pulled herself away from his embrace. She had to think, had to figure this out. "You think the man who fired the first shot was the same man who killed Joseph, don't you, Adam?"

"Yeah," Adam said. "I don't know what else to think. I just want to know why."

"Could be he thinks she can identify him," Elliot said slowly. He paced across Doc's floor, then came back to her again.

"But he knows he was covered head to foot when I saw him. He has to know I couldn't possibly have any clue who he is."

Elliot shrugged. "Maybe you have a clue you aren't aware of."

Adam rubbed her back, soothing the tension that coiled her muscles tight. "Is the pain any better?"

"A little."

"If it comes back, say so. You can take another one of these if you need to." Stepping back a little, he pulled the pill bottle from his pocket, then stood frowning at it. "Hell, I forgot."

"What?" she asked.

Adam glanced at Elliot, then back at her. "This." He handed her the bottle. Not the codeine, but a prescription bottle with Joseph's name on it.

"I found it at your house," Elliot said, coming back to the table where she sat. "It's a narcotic used for pain. A powerful one. Do you have any idea why your husband would have been taking something this potent?"

She shook her head. The movement hurt, and she winced. "No idea at all. I didn't even know he'd seen a doctor...this doctor. Doc's name is on the bottle."

"Yeah," Elliot said, meeting Adam's eyes. "And Doc's files are in the next room."

Adam licked his lips, sent Kirsten a questioning glance.

Kirsten nodded once. "We've come this far. We might as well compound the charges as much as possible, hmm?" Bracing her hands on Adam's shoulders, she slid to the floor. He gripped her waist, steadied her. With his presence and his warmth as much as with his hands. And with the look in his eyes.

"Okay?"

"So long as you hold on to me," she whispered.

He bent, pressed a kiss to her forehead. "Don't worry. I'm not letting go. Not this time."

Elliot cleared his throat and discreetly stepped out into the hallway.

"That's not what I meant," Kirsten said when he'd gone.

"Doesn't matter. It's what I mean."

"But, Adam, you don't know—"

"But I will know. And if you think this deep, dark secret of yours is going to make a difference to me, you're wrong. But you're not going to realize that until you open up to me, Kirsten. Give me the chance to show you that I'll stand by you this time." He squeezed her waist, looked down at her. She couldn't hold his gaze. Guilt twisted her heart up in knots. Adam sighed softly. "But I guess I have to wait until you're ready to tell me. Come on, Elliot's waiting."

He led her into the hall, placed her hand on the wall and let go of her long enough to go to the door, where Elliot was already at work.

The younger Brand jimmied the lock on Doc's office door. Then he swung it open. "Yesss," Elliot whispered with a flourish.

"I don't even want to know where you learned that particular skill," Adam said. He put his arm around Kirsten's shoulders and guided her inside. "Sit here," he said, easing her into the soft chair near Doc's desk. Then he turned to the file cabinet, tinkered with the drawer and finally got it open while Elliot looked on.

"I see I'm not the only one in the family with a talent for criminal acts," Elliot quipped when Adam slid the drawer open.

"Yeah. Must be from those outlaw ancestors of ours, hmm?"

Elliot grinned and leaned closer, while Adam began pawing the files. Kirsten couldn't sit still as Adam thumbed through the folders and finally pulled one out. Pushing herself to her feet, she moved unsteadily closer. Adam had flipped the folder open, was reading slowly. Elliot was leaning over him, reading as well. They looked at each other, and almost in unison the two Brands swore softly.

Kirsten gripped Adam's arm. "What is it? What does it say?"

Licking his lips, Adam looked down at the sheets in front of him. "Carcinoma. Inoperable. Prognosis, terminal." Then he met her eyes. "Cancer," he said softly. "Doc gave Joseph two months at the outside. And this is dated six weeks ago."

It took a moment for the words to sink in, for their meaning to become clear to her. "Joseph…had cancer? He was *dying?* But Adam, how could I not know something like that?"

Adam sighed, flipped a page, read on. "Doc made some notes here. It doesn't sound as if the end was going to be pretty. Says he was concerned the patient might resort to suicide."

"It looks like it was a fast-moving disease," Elliot said. "And with the Percodan, the symptoms might have been tough to spot. Especially if…well, I take it you two didn't spend a whole lot of quality time together. I can't believe Doc thought that old goat was capable of suicide, though. He was too mean...." Elliot looked up fast. "I mean...sorry, Kirsten, I didn't mean..."

"He was mean, all right," she said. Closing her eyes, lowering her head, Kirsten whispered, "But that's just what he did. He killed himself, but he hated me so much, he set me up to take the blame. He's framing me for murder, even though he's already dead by his own damn hand. I knew it. I *knew* it."

Adam met Elliot's eyes, and Elliot shook his head. "That can't be right," he said. "I've read the police files on this—"

"And just how the hell did you manage that?" Adam asked.

Elliot dismissed the question with a scowl and a shake of his head. "The point is, I did. And this can't have been a suicide. Kirsten, they checked Joseph's hands for powder traces. There was no sign. And there would have been—make no mistake, there *would have been*—if he'd fired that gun. Besides, his prints weren't on the weapon."

"Then he wore gloves." She spoke levelly, firmly, not an ounce of doubt in her mind.

"And took them off and got rid of them...*after* putting a bullet into his own head?" Elliot shook his head. "Don't you see how impossible that is?"

"Then he had help." She lifted her head, looked Elliot squarely in the eye. "And that help *wasn't* me. Do you believe me, Elliot?"

Elliot swallowed hard, looked at his brother, then back at Kirsten again. "Yes. I do. But I wouldn't count on that for much, Kirsten. I always was a sucker for a pair of pretty brown eyes."

He was trying to lift her spirits with his charm and his infectious smile. Elliot the lighthearted, practical joker. Always kidding. Always upbeat.

She was grateful for the effort, but it was falling on sterile ground this time. She turned her question on Adam now. "And what about you? Do you believe me now, Adam? Do you believe that Joseph is the one who set this up to make me look guilty?"

He nodded without hesitation. "You know I believe you. But it brings up another question, doesn't it, Kirsty?" She just watched him, waiting. "Why did he hate you that much? What the hell reason would Joseph have to hate you so very much that his dying wish was to see you convicted of his murder? And why is someone—his accomplice, maybe—trying to kill you now?"

"Ease up on her, Adam." Elliot's voice was anything but jovial.

"Why, Kirsten? Think. There has to be something, some motive—"

"I don't know. Dammit, Adam, I don't know." Turning away, she moved back to the chair, her knees so watery she wasn't certain she would be able to stand much longer. "Unless..."

"Unless what?" Adam carried the files to the copy machine, flicked a button, lifted the lid, all the while keeping one eye on Kirsten.

"Unless he found out…about the birth control pills. The one thing he wanted was an heir. A child. And…now that I know about his illness, I guess I can understand why he was so desperate about it. But I couldn't let him win that round. I wouldn't.''

"I know,'' Adam said slowly.

She blinked, thought back. When had she told him any of this? "Another thing I talk about too much when I drink?'' she asked.

Grim faced, he nodded.

"I went out of town for the pills, kept them hidden in the house. He…he was so determined. Especially in the last few weeks…'' She stopped speaking when she saw the way Adam stilled, the way he clenched his hands into fists at his sides, so tightly his knuckles went white.

"I should have killed him myself,'' he whispered.

"I'd gladly have helped,'' Elliot said, his voice deep and quaking.

Kirsten shook her head. "I got myself into this situation. There was nothing either of you could have done. But if Joseph finally realized I'd been taking the pills all along…it would have infuriated him.''

"Enough to do this?'' Adam asked.

She looked up, ashamed. "He was a monster, Adam. No one crossed Joseph Cowan without paying dearly. No one. He told me that again and again. And as many times as he proved it to me, I can't for the life of me figure out why I still thought I could best him.''

Adam nodded, his face grim. "Then we've found his motive."

"And eliminated mine. If he were dying anyway, then I wouldn't have needed to kill him in order to claim the inheritance, would I?"

"I wish it were that simple," Adam said. "But if you didn't know about the illness, it's a moot point. And besides, we both know you had another reason to want him dead. The thing he held over you, the thing he used to blackmail you into that sham of a marriage in the first place."

She looked away quickly. "The police don't know about that. And...and if we put things back the way they were, if we're careful, they won't know we were ever here, either. I can say I knew about the illness all along."

"More lies, Kirsten? You really think you can fix all of this with even more lies?"

She lowered her head, drew a shaky breath.

"Dammit, Adam, let up on her," Elliot said, raising his voice. "I'd lie like a rug if it were me!"

"They'd only ask why she didn't tell them about Cowan's illness in the first place. Why she ran. And last I knew, assisted suicides were still illegal. And that's what they'd say this was. They'd still charge her with murder, even if she could convince them it was all Cowan's idea. Because she's still the one whose prints are on the weapon."

Her body slumped. Every word Adam spoke robbed her of more strength, until she didn't feel she could even get out of the chair.

"He's right, Elliot," she said at last. "Your brother is right."

"My brother is brutal." Elliot came to the chair and knelt in front of her. "We're gonna get you out of this mess, Kirsten. You hang tough, okay? Don't give up yet. I'll take you to Mexico myself if it comes to that, you hear me?"

She smiled at Elliot. So strong. So much a Brand man, through and through. "Thanks for that." Leaning forward, she kissed his cheek. "It means a lot, Elliot. If I'd had a brother like you, I..." Her voice trailed off, and she shook her head slowly.

"You do have," he said, and he squeezed her hand.

Adam finished with the copies, returned the file to the drawer. "If you're finished making kissy faces with Kirsten, Elliot, you can take these copies. Show 'em to Garrett and then stash them someplace safe."

Straightening, a little red in the face, Elliot nodded and took the sheaf of papers Adam held out. "All right. You two gonna be okay?" He was talking to Adam, but his eyes were on Kirsten.

She nodded. "Thanks for the help, Elliot. You're a real knight in shining armor."

"Yeah," Adam said. "A real prince. Get your backside home, now, Galahad, before Sir Garrett catches you out here and tosses us both in the dungeon."

Elliot faced his brother. Adam held out a hand. Elliot took it. "Thanks, little brother," Adam said. And his eyes said he meant it.

"Holler if you need me." Elliot let go, tipped his hat to Kirsten and left Doc's office.

Adam sighed, slid the file cabinet drawer closed and faced Kirsten again. "I'm sorry," he said. "Seems like I'm forever saying and doing the wrong thing with you. I just want this to be over. I want this garbage and all the lies out of the way."

"I know."

"I'm just trying to be realistic. Kirsten, it's time for you to wake up and realize that the only way out of this is for you to tell the truth. All of it. And you can start by telling it to me."

His face swam because of the tears in her eyes. "I know that, too."

"I'll understand. I promise, whatever you might have done, it isn't going to make a difference in the way I feel about you."

Her smile was bitter. She closed her eyes, unable to look at the pain and the love in his any longer. "It will," she said. "But maybe there's just no way around that. I have to face it. And when I do, I'm going to lose you all over again, Adam."

"You won't. God, I hate to see you hurting like this. It's killing me not to be able to take away that pain in your eyes."

"Do you really want to take this pain away for me, Adam?"

He stared at her, a puzzled frown bending his brows. "You know I do. I'd take it on myself if I could." He knelt in front of her and gathered her close in his arms. Dropping soft kisses in her hair, he kneaded her shoulders and spoke softly. ''I'd take away every bad thing that's ever happened to you, sweetheart. If you'd just tell me how.''

A shuddering sob worked its way out of her, and she nodded against his chest. ''Okay,'' she whispered. ''I'll tell you how.''

Adam went still, not moving, waiting for her to go on, she knew.

''Take me away from here, Adam. Take me someplace...soft...and dark...and make love to me, one last time. You were the first, and I want you to be the last. Maybe all that happened in between will stop haunting me then. And in the morning I'll tell you what you want to know. And you'll hate me, and it will be over...for you. But I'll have one sweet memory to hold on to. And I'll cherish it, no matter what else happens. I'll be able to face the rest, the truth, all of it, if I can just have this one night to be with you.''

He leaned away slightly, searching her face. ''You can have as many nights with me as you want, lady. But it won't be like you think it's going to be. Have a little faith in me, Kirsty.''

''I have all the faith in the world in you, Adam. But that's the way it will be.''

''I—''

She pressed a finger to his lips. ''No. Don't talk about the secrets I have to tell you. Not now. Not again, not until morning. Promise me.''

He probed her eyes for a long time. And finally he nodded. ''Okay. Okay, Kirsty. I won't talk. I'll show you instead.'' And then he kissed her. Long, and slow, and deep. When he stood, he took her with him, scooping her up into his arms. And then he carried her out of Doc's tiny office and into the night.

Adam carried her into the hay-scented barn at the west side of town and up the ladder into the loft. It was dark in here, dusty and warm. It smelled good. Fresh and clean. He lowered her into the hay. It scratched the denim she wore and pillowed her aching head. She could hear the horses in the barn below them, where Adam had put them for the night.

He came down beside her, ran a hand through her hair. "Kirsty, do you know where we are?"

Her throat tightened just a little. She nodded, but she doubted he could see her in the darkness. All she could see of him was the tiny gleam of light shining in his eyes. The rest of him was just a darker shadow among shadows. "It's the Recknor place, isn't it?"

"Yeah. Do you remember the first time I brought you here?"

Tears tried to choke her. She'd been seventeen. He'd been eighteen. And they'd both been holding themselves in check for way longer than any of their friends. Until one day after school, when they'd sneaked into old man Recknor's hayloft. It was too private, too intimate, too safe, to keep them from exploring further.

"I couldn't see you," Adam whispered. "Just like now. It was so dark, I had to look at you with my hands. I had to feel how perfect you were. How right."

"I remember," she whispered.

Adam pushed the denim shirt down her arms, and his palms, hot and callused, skimmed her flesh. He ran his hands over her T-shirt, cupping her breasts, squeezing her and releasing his breath in a shaky sigh. "I've made love to you a thousand times in the past two years," he told her. "In my mind. In my sleep. My pillow becomes your face." He pushed the T-shirt up, baring her breasts to the cool night air. Then he touched them again, rough palms on tender crests. Shrill sensation clawed through her. "I'd bring the sheets to my lips and imagine these breasts. I'd touch myself and imagine your body."

"Adam," she whispered. "I swear I never wanted anyone but you. Never..."

"There hasn't *been* anyone but me," he told her. "Not in any way that matters." He kissed and suckled her breasts, then her throat, then her jaw and cheek. "Let the time melt away, Kirsty. It's been you and me all along. I think we both know that." He moved his hand to the zipper of her jeans and slid it slowly down. When he slipped his hand inside, she arched against his touch.

"I haven't been alive without you," he told her, kissing her, speaking brokenly, passionately, against her lips, against her skin. "And you haven't, either. Neither of us has existed without the other. So nothing that happened was real. None of it matters. None of it exists. Just this. Just us, Kirsty. Just this life that only lives when we're together."

He shoved her jeans down and moved to cover her body with his own. She felt him there, hard and real, and she believed everything he was saying to her. That this was all that mattered, all that was real. That nothing in between had ever really happened. That right now was their forever.

Adam slid inside her, and she closed her eyes, twisted her arms tight around him and held on. She loved this man. She could never love any other. It was him; it was only him.

He completed her.

"I love you, Kirsty," he whispered. "I never stopped. I never will."

He pushed her to the edge, then over, and when she spiraled downward, he caught her and began carrying her up again. He made love to her over and over again that night. And she didn't want it to end. She didn't ever want it to end. Because when it did...it would end forever.

Chapter 10

Dread. The feeling hit him along about the time he stirred awake and noticed the soft dawn beams that poked their way through the cracks in the barn walls and painted pale amber stripes on Kirsten's face, in her hair and across the fragrant hay around her. It was morning. The morning when she had promised she would tell him her deepest secrets…and *he* had promised that those secrets would make no earthly difference to him.

A cold fist closed around his belly and squeezed. A deep burn traced the path of his sternum and spread its wings into his chest. As he sat up, staring down at Kirsten and wondering what the hell was happening to his logical, strategy-prone mind, she moved closer. A soft moan in protest of his absence, before she snuggled against him, nestled her head into his chest. And the sensations raging through him intensified. His heart went into meltdown, and his pulse seemed erratic and electrified. His scalp tingled. His spine shivered. He was alternately hot as hell and cold all over.

He'd done it, then, hadn't he? He'd conjured up the kind of love he hadn't been able to feel for Kirsten before. The kind he had always secretly known she deserved. An all-consuming, sickening, bigger-than-life kind of love. The kind Garrett and Chelsea had found with each other. The kind Ben and Penny had cherished and nurtured from the time they were schoolkids. The kind that had turned his hot-tempered brother Wes into a pussycat and had turned peace-loving Lash Monroe into a tiger, ready to take on all his lady's big brothers, if that was what it took to win her heart.

Adam loved Kirsten in a way he had never realized he could love anyone. And it brought a huge shadow of ice-cold fear over his soul. And an old pain came creeping with it. A surge of the feelings he'd kept locked away for a long, long time. Darkness. Heartbreak. Loss. Betrayal. Abandonment. The fear of it happening all over again. The grim certainty that it would. That it would *always* happen to him.

If he lost her, he realized slowly, it was going to destroy him. And he couldn't shake that ingrained belief that he was about to do just that—lose her. He knew where the feeling came from. You take a kid who believes with everything in him that his parents will always be there, and you rob him of that faith…and there is no doubt that kid will lose his faith in everything. In every*one*. In any kind of permanence. It ceases to exist for him from that moment on. He becomes convinced that there is no such thing as for-ever. That, for him, *nothing* good will ever last more than a few brief moments.

Adam didn't want to believe those things, but he couldn't help it any more than he could change the genetic structure of his own DNA. It was too in-grained, too deep. Too well learned.

He was scared, plain and simply scared.

He reached down, his hand trembling, and stroked Kirsten's hair away from her face. She opened her eyes. Met his. Frowned slightly. "Adam?"

"I changed my mind," he said, very softly, barely above a whisper, as he studied her dark lashes and the way they brushed her cheeks when she blinked up at him.

"What?" She blinked the sleep haze from her eyes and sat up, leaning on her elbow. "Changed your mind about what, Adam?"

He tried to swallow and couldn't. "I don't want to know this secret you've been keeping. Don't tell me, Kirsty," he whispered, voice choked, throat tight. "I just don't think I want to know anymore. Maybe I don't *need* to know."

She closed her eyes very slowly, left them closed for a long moment, and drew a deep breath. "You need to know," she said slowly. "It's taken me a while to figure it out, but you do. And I need to tell you. I owe you the truth, Adam. You were right last night when you said it was...the only way out for me.''

He swallowed the lump in his throat. ''I was afraid you'd say something like that.''

''It might just be the only way out for you, too,'' she said, looking into his eyes again. ''The only way you can let go of whatever it is you think you feel for me and move on with your life.''

''Don't do that,'' he said. ''Don't try to make it easier by telling yourself I'm imagining what I feel for you, Kirsten, because we both know that's a lie.''

''Is it?'' She sat up straighter, brushed hay from her hair and reached for her discarded T-shirt. Her bare skin amber in the morning light, she slowly covered herself, and Adam sighed softly as he looked on. ''That's what my father told my mother once, you know,'' she went on. ''I was a kid. Wasn't supposed to be hearing their arguments.'' She laughed bitterly. ''Do you know how many parents think their kids aren't hearing their arguments? What do they think, the sense of hearing develops only during adolescence?''

Sensing this subject was important, that this meant a lot to her and maybe had something to do with the two of them now, Adam moved closer, sat down on a bale of hay and let her talk it through. He didn't know where this was leading, was half afraid to follow her there. But he didn't think he had a choice. ''What were they fighting about?''

She shook her head. ''It was awful. Dad's heart was so bad, even then. Somehow he'd found out that

Mother had done...something in the past. Before they were married. And he kept saying that he loved her, that it didn't matter to him, that all he wanted from her was the truth." Kirsten's lips thinned. "So she gave him the truth."

He could see the remembered pain in her eyes. They were wide, pupils dilated as she remembered. "I was ten. I remember sitting on the stairs, with my hands wrapped around two of the spindles in the railing, and my face peering between them. Mom and Dad were just below, in the living room. He was pacing. She was sitting as still as a statue in the rocking chair. Just like stone. I'll never forget her face. She *knew*. I could see that she knew what would happen. It *was* going to make a difference to him. And I remember, even though I was only ten years old, I sat there thinking as hard as I could at her, *Don't tell him, Mama. Whatever it is, just don't tell him.*"

Sniffling, Kirsten lowered her head, so Adam could no longer see her eyes.

"But she told him anyway, didn't she?" he asked.

Head turned away, Kirsten nodded. "She told him anyway. She said she'd been with another man while she was engaged to marry Daddy. She said this other man had gotten her pregnant. And that when Daddy had believed she was spending a summer in Europe, she'd actually been out of town, making arrangements to get rid of the unwanted child."

Adam reached out, touched her face. "She aborted the baby?"

"I don't know. Those were the words she used.

Cold words that sent a chill right up my spine. 'Get rid of it.' She didn't elaborate on what had become of...my unborn sibling. She never got the chance, really.''

Swallowing against the dryness in his throat—part of his reaction to seeing Kirsten relive such a painful experience—Adam squeezed her hand briefly.

She nodded and went on. "It was obvious my father had known parts of this already. I don't know how he found out, but I think he knew who the man was. I never heard the name, just Daddy, muttering, swearing, calling the man a bastard, using other words I had never heard him use before.''

Adam lowered his head and brought her hand to his lips. He wanted to kiss away the remembered pain, but he knew he couldn't. "I'm sorry, Kirsten.''

"Daddy was devastated. He just kept pacing, faster and faster, and I could see his face going pale, and then ashen. I could tell that something horrible was happening to him. The way he kept yanking at his collar. The way the sweat popped out on his face. Mama got up, went to him, asked what was wrong. And Daddy just rolled his eyes back in his head and sank to the floor.''

"My God,'' Adam whispered. "It was his first heart attack, wasn't it?''

Kirsten nodded. "He'd been seeing a cardiologist. We knew his heart was bad. Until then, he'd only had a few episodes of angina. But this...it was massive. It did a lot of damage, and he never really recovered from it.''

Adam could see it all so vividly in his mind. Kirsten, small, innocent, seeing her hero fall like that. Her face peering from between the spindles on the stairway, big brown eyes stricken as she witnessed a nightmare that would bring an adult to tears.

"I ran to him," she said, her voice having gone softer than the smallest whisper. "I went a little crazy just then, I think. I kept screaming, shaking him, crying. I was hysterical. And I shouted things at my mother. Things I never should have said. Things no child should ever say, or even think of saying, to a parent. I told her I hated her. I told her that this was all her fault, that if my father died, I would never forgive her."

Tears flowed silently from Kirsten's eyes now. Slow and shiny as glycerin, they slid down her cheeks.

"She called an ambulance for my father. And took me with her to the hospital. And she stayed...all night, she stayed. But the minute the doctors told us that Daddy was going to live, she left us there. And I never saw her again."

Adam lowered his head. Such heartache was tough to get past, tough to deal with. Tougher not to, though. "And you blamed yourself for her leaving? Blamed it on the things you had said to her?"

Kirsten looked him in the eyes, and hers were red and wet. "For a while. But I realize now it wasn't entirely my fault. It wasn't even entirely *her* fault. She made a mistake in her past, and then she hid it from the man she loved. She knew what was going to happen when she told him the truth. She'd always known.

And all those years they had together, she must have realized that sooner or later the day would come when she would have to tell him. She must have known. It must have eaten away at her soul every minute of every day. I just never realized that…until it happened to me.''

''Kirsten—''

''I didn't sleep with another man, or have a child I never told you about, Adam. What I did was far worse. Far worse. And I know, just as my mother knew, that when I tell you—'' sighing, she lowered her head ''—it's going to change everything. The way you look at me. The way you feel about me. Everything.''

Drawing a deep breath, Kirsten got to her feet. She seemed to test her balance, then touched her fingertips gingerly to her bandaged head.

''Is it hurting again?'' Adam asked. Maybe to delay the inevitable. To change the subject. He wanted to keep on insisting that whatever she was about to say would make no difference to him, but he was afraid now. So afraid…that maybe it would.

''It's a lot better than it was last night.'' She reached for her jeans, stepped into them and pulled them up. Already he could feel the distance yawning wider between them. She seemed to be putting it there. Deliberately.

He watched as she tucked her shirt carefully into her jeans, then zipped and buttoned them. She pulled on the denim shirt then, rolling the sleeves, straightening the collar. Then she finger-combed her hair. Adam thought that, if she could, maybe she would be slapping on a coat of makeup right now, and hiding herself behind some expensive designer suit.

He wished they could go back to last night. Make that time go on longer. Forever, maybe. He wished he didn't have to face this thing, because he'd never known Kirsten to exaggerate. He wished he had a cup of coffee. Or, better yet, a stiff drink.

She finished doing what she could with her hair and went still. Nothing more to do. No more time to kill. She stood there staring at him for a moment, as if drinking in the sight of him. And then she looked away from him and closed her eyes. Took a deep breath. When the words came, they were forced, clipped and short.

"I was fourteen. No driver's license. No clue. I took Daddy's car without permission. Went joyriding. There was an accident. It was my fault."

Her jaw was tight as she spoke. He could almost feel her teeth grating between the words. Was that all? An accident? For just an instant a hint of relief began to ease his knotted muscles, despite the tension in her voice, her stance, her very breath. She stood so still, so rigidly. She was like a sculpture. Like the way she'd described her mother. Golden stripes of sunlight crisscrossed her body in the middle of the dusty, hay-strewn barn. Her hair was loose and flowing. But she stood utterly still. Venus in blue jeans. And for just that brief instant he thought that was all, and that it wasn't as bad as she'd made him believe.

"Fourteen?" he heard himself ask. "This terrible

secret you've been keeping happened when you were only fourteen?''

She nodded. ''Joseph Cowan was in the car behind me with that odd, quiet driver of his…Phillip Carr. The two of them rushed me away from the scene before I really even got it clear in my head what had happened. By the time I did, I was at the estate.''

So stiff. Forcing the words out as fast as she could, barely pausing for a breath. ''You left the scene?'' Adam asked. She didn't seem to hear him.

''Joseph said I should forget it had ever happened. He and Phillip had checked on the people in the other car, and they told me they were fine. Shaken up, too shaken to remember me…what I was driving or…or anything else…but otherwise, fine. Joseph said there was no harm done. That he and Phillip would take care of everything. Inside an hour, my father's car had been repaired. It was as if nothing had happened, and Joseph took me home. And I thought it really was for the best.''

Adam shook his head. ''I don't understand. Why would a man like Cowan want to help a fourteen-year-old kid cover up an accident?''

She glanced at Adam briefly. ''He knew what he was doing. He knew who I was, who my father was. He and my father…they never got along. But I didn't know any of that at the time. I just agreed, did what he said. Because of my father…his heart, you know… I thought it would be better for him if I just went along with Joseph's plan. Acted like none of it had ever happened. I kept picturing myself telling him that I'd taken his car out and caused an accident. Picturing his face going gray and sweaty like it had four years before, when my mother had damned near killed him with her confession..."

She finally stopped for a breath. Adam moved closer to her. The relief he'd felt before was fading. Because she wasn't finished. He knew she wasn't. The worst was yet to come. It flickered like the flames of hell in her eyes. She was still dreading the end.

"There...has to be more to it than that," he said softly. She said nothing.

"Kirsten?"

She stared into his eyes for a long, tense moment, and he could almost see her heart breaking. No. It had already broken...a long, long time ago. He was only just now identifying that change in her once lively eyes. "Tell me the rest."

She had to look away. Whatever it was, it was bad enough that she couldn't tell him while looking him in the eye.

Dust motes danced in the sunbeams between them. Like the small lies that had kept them apart all this time.

"Joseph lied to me that day. I never knew. Not until years later. After we'd moved here to Quinn, my daddy and I. After I'd met you and fallen...fallen in love with you." She bit her lip. "I never learned what really happened on that stretch of Highway 5 until our wedding day."

Her words shook Adam to the marrow. But he

didn't move. Didn't speak. He just stood still in the hay, waiting.

"Joseph came to my house that day. Daddy had suffered a minor episode with his heart the night before, and he was resting at the hospital. I was shaken up about that. I hadn't called you yet to tell you about it, because Daddy had insisted I not interrupt the bachelor party your brothers were throwing for you over at La Cucaracha. I was about to call you, to tell you about it. And that Daddy probably wouldn't be able to come to our wedding, but he was insisting we go on with it all the same. But then Joseph came. Didn't knock, just walked in. I was standing in my bedroom in front of a triple mirror I'd bought just so I could be sure I looked all right. I was wearing my wedding gown. I looked..." A sigh stuttered from her lungs. "Oh, Adam, I wish you could have seen me. Daddy was okay. His doctors had assured me it had been a minor episode. And I was about to live out my fantasy. I was more alive, standing there, wearing that gown, thinking of the day ahead...than I'd ever been in my life. And far more than I have been since."

She licked her lips, lowered her head. "Except, maybe, for last night."

She met his eyes, held them, and for just a second the fire flared between them again. Then she looked quickly away. Impatience nipped at Adam's heels, but he tried to keep it from coming through in his tone. He was angry. The thought of Cowan, that bastard, going to Kirsten on the day she was to marry Adam... He wanted to kill him. "What did he say to you?"

"He said that I wasn't going to marry you, Adam. He said that I was going to marry him instead, that very day. That he needed a young, pretty, trophy wife. One who could be controlled, manipulated, counted on to keep her silence when necessary, and capable of producing an heir, which was his main goal. He made it sound as if it had already been decided. As if there was no question of my refusing him. He said he'd gone over all of his options and had chosen me. That I should thank my lucky stars. That I was about to become Quinn's newest millionaire."

She lifted her head, staring up at the dark, splintering beams that crisscrossed above. A swallow swooped and dived, and she never even blinked. "I laughed at him. Thought he was joking, at first. I hadn't seen him in all that time, not since I was fourteen years old. But then I realized he was serious, and I asked him how he planned to make me do such a thing. Why I would even consider marrying a man I didn't even know, much less love—a man old enough to be my father—when my beloved was even now waiting at the chapel for me."

Slowly, she lowered her head.

"And he said that if you didn't do what he wanted," Adam filled in slowly, "he would turn you in for an accident that had happened all those years earlier." He shook his head. "Did you really think it would be that big a deal? That you'd go to jail over a teenage lapse in judgment?"

"Of course not. And that's exactly what I told him." She turned now, and seemingly by sheer force

of will, she faced him. "And then he told me the rest."
Her knees bent just a little, but she snapped them
straight again. "The people in the other car were not
okay, Adam. Joseph told me they were at the time,
just to make sure I'd go along with what he wanted.
So he'd be able to hold it over my head later. He did
that, you know. Collected things like that…things he
could use to own the souls of the people who had been
unlucky enough to cross his path. Some he never used.
Some came in handy later. Years later, in my case."

Adam blinked, staring back at her as intensely as
she was staring at him. "The people in the other
car…were hurt?"

Unblinking, chin quivering, she whispered, "Dead.
They were dead."

Adam's eyes slammed closed, even as he instinctively reached for her. His hands closed on her shoulders, offering comfort, support. "My God," he whispered. "Oh, my God."

Gently she took his hands away. "Joseph said I
would go to prison if he turned me in. He'd kept the
evidence. Photos somehow taken at the scene without
my knowledge. God knows I was so shaken at the time
that I wouldn't have noticed Phillip snapping them,
anyway. The documentation of the quick repairs made
to my father's car. His own testimony as an eyewit-
ness."

Adam lowered his head. So she'd chosen to break
his heart, desert him and marry a man she didn't love
just to avoid prosecution. Hardly a noble motive. But
honest, at least. He wouldn't have expected it of her.

"I told him to go ahead. Told him I didn't care if I ended up in prison, that I wouldn't leave you standing at the altar without a bride. I couldn't bear to do that to you."

Slowly, Adam's head came up. "But you *did* do that to me."

"Yes," she said. "I did. Because he told me the rest of it then. He told me my relationship with you was over anyway. That even if I refused him, I'd never have you. That you'd hate me before that day was out, one way or another. Either because I stood you up, or because you learned what I had done."

"And you believed him? You believed I'd hate you because of an accident that happened when you were barely out of middle school?"

She held his gaze for a long moment; then her face crumpled, and she squeezed her eyes tight. Tears worked through anyway. "I believed him because he told me the names of the people in the other car. The people my...my carelessness, my *recklessness,* had— had—had destroyed." Sobs came like hiccups now. Her chest rose and fell in staccato breaths, and her words came in broken whispers. "They were...they were..." Head down, palms to temples, eyes tight. "Orrin and Maria Brand."

Adam didn't hear her. He just kept looking at her, while the words she'd spoken took the slow path to his brain. To his awareness. To his conscious mind. And then he interpreted them. And every ounce of blood seemed to drain to his toes.

"My parents?" he whispered. "My *parents?* Oh,

my God, Kirsten, it was *you?* You killed my mother and father?'' His legs went out from under him. His backside slammed down onto a bale of hay, and his head spun. He couldn't look at her. She was rushing on, spinning explanations.

''I never knew, Adam. I would never have kept it from you if I'd known.''

He sat there, head in his hands, stunned and blinking in shock, as a swirling storm of memories attacked him from every direction.

''I never would have let Joseph cover up the accident if I had known that people had been hurt...that people had...had been killed.'' Kirsten paced away, pushing her hands through her hair. ''But I didn't know. Joseph...he lied. He cajoled and convinced me that his way was for the best. I was just young enough and naive enough to let myself be convinced. Because it was easier that way. It was the biggest mistake I ever made, Adam. And I've been regretting it ever since.''

He didn't look up when she paused, though he could feel her eyes on him. She came closer. He felt her. She put a hand on his shoulder.

He flinched away from her touch. And he heard the pained gasp that was her reaction.

''When Joseph came to me on our wedding day and told me what I'd done...I knew he was right about one thing, Adam. You were going to hate me either way. So my choice then wasn't whether or not to go through with our wedding. Because Joseph would have seen to it that you knew, and the wedding was never going to happen. My choice was whether to let you hate me for standing you up at the altar, or to let you hate me for murdering your parents.''

Gasping for enough air to fuel his words, he managed, ''Exactly. That was your choice. And you made the wrong one.''

''Joseph helped me make the wrong one,'' she said. ''I'm not excusing what I did. But I had to act quickly, Adam, and I was totally in shock. Utterly devastated. Horrified at learning I'd not only killed two people, but that they were the parents of the man I loved. Learning only hours before what I had thought would be the happiest moment of my life that it was never going to happen.

''Joseph said that he knew about my father's health. He said that if the truth about the accident ever came out, it would kill Daddy. Kill him. And he was right, Adam. Daddy was already bad enough that he needed in-home care, a nurse on call.''

''Oh, I know. I remember.'' His voice was thin, harsh. ''We planned for that, don't you remember, Kirsten? Don't you remember all those ridiculous dreams? We were going to buy the biggest ranch around and turn it into a resort. A dude ranch with mock cattle drives and camp-outs for the customers. We were going to have plenty of room for Max. He would have been in his glory playing cowboy in full costume. We were going to give him a role to play in our lives, in our business. Make him feel needed, keep him active and vital. Do you remember all that, Kirsten? All the nights we spent talking, making plans?''

She nodded, looking almost too tired to hold her head up. "I remember everything."

"You threw those plans away. Instead of playing cowboy, Max Armstrong is living out his days in a nursing home with a yard the size of a dog kennel and nary a horse nor a Stetson in sight. All because his little girl didn't want to confess that she was less than perfect to a father who idolized her. Isn't that what it really comes down to, Kirsten?"

She lifted her head, met his eyes. "Is that what you really believe?"

He looked into Kirsten's brown wounded eyes and shook his head. "I don't really know what the hell I believe anymore."

"Believe this," she whispered. "This lie has been eating me up inside for a long time now. It's been killing me to keep it from you. It had to come out, Adam, and no matter what happens from here on in, I'm glad it finally did. At least...at least you know the truth now," she whispered.

Tears burned behind his eyes. But he knew they wouldn't spill over. They never had. Never. His throat went so tight he could barely pull air through it. His lungs spasmed painfully. "What I don't understand is how you could have kept something like this from me for as long as you have, Kirsten."

"Joseph promised prison for me if I told. He promised to let my father know exactly where I was, even to fly him in for my trial. He swore Daddy wouldn't last through the D.A.'s opening statement, and I knew he was right, Adam. I had no choice."

He looked up, his eyes narrowed. "You *always* had a choice. The choice was to trust me."

Unable to argue with that, she looked away.

He made a sound of disgust in his throat, yanked up his hat and slammed it down on his head. He needed to escape. He needed to run. *Now.* "I'm out of here. You made this mess on your own, Kirsten— you can just get out of it the same way. I've given up enough for you. *My family* has given up enough for you. No more." He was striking back, returning pain for pain, he knew that. It didn't stop him from doing it anyway.

He headed for the barn door, lifted the crosspiece, shoved it open. Sunlight spilled blindingly onto his face, heated him through his clothes. He smelled grass, freshly cut. And grain and cattle. He stood still, some small part of him knowing he shouldn't keep going. Some kernel of sanity telling him to slow down. To digest this shock and think it through and not just storm off this way. To pause and think first.

"It's all right," she said from behind him. "I knew you'd walk away once I told you the truth. I've been expecting it, Adam, and I don't blame you. I deserve it. I deserve worse. I ought to go to prison for murder, and I know that. If it wasn't for Daddy, I'd stand up like I ought to and face the music. But for his sake, I have to wait.... I have to let him go on believing in me...just for a little bit longer."

"You do whatever you have to, Kirsten. I don't give a damn anymore."

Even as he said it, though, he knew it was a lie. But

he stomped away, all the same. He left her alone. Walked off in a temper just the way he'd done two years before when she'd left him standing there in the chapel, alone. A groom without a bride. Looking and feeling like the biggest fool in Texas. Only it was different this time. Because this time his love for her went deeper. It went clear to his soul this time. And it hurt ten times more than it ever had before. He should have stayed the hell away from her. Kirsten had never been anything but trouble to him and his, and she never would be.

Chapter 11

Kirsten watched him leave. He walked for a time along the dusty, early-morning street of the tiny west Texas town. Then he ran. As if he couldn't get away from her fast enough. When he rounded a corner and vanished from sight, she lowered her head and let the tears come. She'd known what to expect. She had always known he wouldn't love her anymore once he knew the truth. She had been preparing herself for this very reaction from him for two years now. So why did it still come as such a shattering blow? Why the hell did it hurt so much? Was there truly some stupid, naive little girl inside her who had believed his reaction would be...*could be*...any different?

What had she expected? That Adam would take her into his arms and whisper that he forgave her? That he would tell her it wasn't her fault, that he didn't hate her for what she'd done?

That he still loved her?

"Grow up, little girl," she whispered to herself. Angrily she backhanded hot tears from her eyes. "Okay. So it's time. Time to figure out what the hell to do. Time to face the consequences of my actions, once and for all. God knows it's long overdue."

Pushing her hair into some semblance of control, wishing to God she had a makeup kit or a hairbrush nearby, she stepped back into the dimness of the barn and walked to the far end, where the horses stood contentedly munching hay. As if the whole world hadn't just collapsed around them. As if everything were as fine and normal as it had been before.

She saddled them both and led them outside. She would return them to Wes…or see to it someone did. Soon. First things first, though. She had no time to grieve, no time to mourn. It was time to act. She had no reason to stay in Texas a moment longer. No reason at all. She would make just one stop before she made her way out of Quinn forever. One stop to nurture the small hope that maybe…just maybe…a clue had turned up somewhere. One that pointed to someone else having put that bullet between Joseph Cowan's eyes.

She almost wished it *had* been her.

She mounted Mystic, the mare she'd been riding since she and Adam had left Sky Dancer Ranch with the borrowed pair, and led the other horse, Layla, along beside her. Riding around behind the barn to avoid Quinn's main street, she kept watch but saw little activity. She took to a trail that ran behind most of the shops and businesses in town. She would be less visible that way. She didn't have far to go. Stephen Hawkins' law office was in his home, and that was just a half mile away.

She didn't know why the hell she was wasting her time, taking this chance. She should just run for it, now, before it was too late. But damn the still small voice inside her head—the one that kept whispering that she had to make sure.

Sure of what?

Sure that there was no hope. Sure that it was all over, that leaving was her only option.

And sure that Adam really meant what he'd said— that he wanted nothing more to do with her. Because if she hung around just a little while longer, gave him time to think it through, he might just change his mind.

And letting herself believe that was probably the most self-destructive thing she'd done yet, and that was saying something.

She drew the horses to a stop in the backyard of Stephen Hawkins' small house, took a wary look around and saw no one. In fact, it was so quiet and still, it was eerie. The curtains of the tiny house were drawn tight, and not a single light shone from within. But the tin-can strains of a radio made their way from somewhere inside the dim house.

She looped both mares' reins around a low-hanging limb and walked closer. The back door stood at the top of a small set of steps. Beside them a bird feeder was mounted atop a pole. But no birds were hanging out there today. She didn't even hear any singing.

She walked up the steps, pulled open the screen door, tapped on the wooden one. While she waited for an answer, she identified the song playing from inside. Not a radio. A record album, from the sounds of it. An old Hank Williams tune, skipping and playing the same broken, fragmented line over and over again.

Something twisted in Kirsten's belly, and she knocked again. As she did, she sent a sideways glance toward the driveway at the side of the house. She could see the front fender of Stephen's car. So he was here, then. Maybe just not up yet.

Yeah. Maybe he's sleeping through that incessantly skipping record.

She pounded harder on the door. "Stephen?" she called. "Are you here?"

No answer. Swallowing what felt like a coating of sand on her throat, she tried the knob, and it gave. When she let it go, the door swung slowly open, and Kirsten stepped inside. One step, a glance to the left, a glance to the right...

Big mistake.

Stephen Hawkins was hanging limply from a rope, just above the kitchen table. It was tied to the light fixture up there. On the floor behind him, the chair he'd used to help him kill himself lay toppled on its back. His face was mottled, mouth agape, tongue...

She turned away as the scream ripped from her chest and filled the entire house.

Running footsteps came from outside, up the back

steps, and then a man was gripping her shoulders, looking past her, swearing softly.

Elliot Brand.

He tucked her head to his chest, anchoring her there with a solid arm around her shoulders, and he took her outside, away from the horror.

She didn't know what the hell Adam's brother was doing there...she was just glad he was.

"It's okay," he was saying. "It's okay."

She couldn't stop shaking, couldn't stop her teeth from chattering.

Elliot hugged her against him as he walked away from the house. He put her on one of the horses, climbed up behind her, put his arms around her waist.

"We...we can't just leave him...like that," she whispered.

"I'll call Garrett. But before I do that, I need to stash you someplace safe. Where the hell is Adam? What is he thinking, letting you wander around town all alone, anyway?"

He looked down at her as he asked the question, nudging the horse into gear, wrapping the other one's reins around the pommel even as they lurched into motion.

"He...I..." She choked on her tears. "He's gone. He hates me now."

"Bull."

"It's not bull. You will, too, soon enough."

"Now I *know* that's bull. Where is he, hon?"

She swallowed hard. "Last I saw him, he was headed toward the Badlands, out where they almost meet the road off the north edge of town. He was…he was pretty upset. I hurt him, Elliot.''

"He'll be all right.''

"I hope so.''

"He's a Brand. He'll be all right.'' He kicked the horse into a canter and maneuvered them away from the main roads, cutting across back lawns and fields until they got to the other side of town.

"Here we are.'' Elliot stopped the horses and helped her to the ground. They were looking back on Jessi Brand's Veterinary Clinic and the neat cottage beside it. "Jess isn't back yet,'' Elliot explained. "You'll be safe here until I take care of this whole mess.'' He dug in his pocket for a key, ushered her inside his sister's home and closed the door behind them. Then he snatched up the phone and punched numbers.

Kirsten looked around. The place was cozy. Earth tones and lots of hardwood. A rocking chair with a ruffled cushion, where Jessi Brand probably spent happy hours rocking her little girl, while her loving husband looked on adoringly.

Envy twisted like a blade in her belly. She would never know that kind of normalcy or comfort…or love. The only things that surrounded her were ugly things. Death and fear and lies. She couldn't believe that was ever likely to change.

"Garrett,'' Elliot was saying into the receiver. "You'd better get out to Stephen Hawkins' place. He's dead. Looks like a suicide.''

There was a loud response from the other end, but

Elliot interrupted. "No time now. Just get out there. I'll talk to you later." And Elliot hung up.

He turned to Kirsten, gripped her shoulders and eased her into a soft, overstuffed chair. "Now I have to go check on Adam. But I'll be back soon. Are you gonna be all right?"

She nodded, but it was false. She didn't feel all right. She felt dazed and disoriented and pretty well devastated to boot.

"Yeah, sure you are. You're the furthest thing from all right. You just stay put, lady. Okay? You just curl up here...." He pushed her a little, gently, until she lay back in the chair. Then he pulled a blanket from the back of it and tucked it around her. "Just rest here until I get back, okay?"

She nodded.

Elliot stood there looking at her for a long moment. "That brother of mine is some kind of fool to have left you behind."

"No," she whispered. "No. Leaving me was the smartest thing he ever did."

Adam kept walking, heading away from the barn where he'd taken her, where they'd spent the night. The place where that barn sat—the old Recknor ranch—was one of the places he and Kirsten had once thought of buying together. It was one of the places they'd talked about refurbishing, turning into their dude ranch. It was also the first place they had made love, that big, shadowy old barn.

And it was the place where it had all fallen apart,

at long last. About two years overdue, that breakdown. But it had happened in the same place where they had first begun to learn from each other what love was.

Ironic.

He would never go back to that barn again. Never. He would never even drive by the Recknor place again, if he could help it. It ate at his pride to think he had been stupid enough to let some of those old dreams slip back into his mind, his heart. To think he had been gullible enough to hope, even for a minute, that they could come true after all.

He headed out toward the desert, walking faster with every step, then running. All-out, long, powerful strides. The wind swept his hat off and sent it tumbling through the dust behind him, but he didn't give a damn. He ran until the hot Texas sun sizzled on his skin and the sweat ran into his eyes and stung and burned. The pain was good. He ran until his legs screamed and his muscles ached and his head swam and his lungs begged. And then he ran some more. He wanted the pain. He wanted the exhaustion. Anything to drown out the sound of his heart breaking. Anything to squelch the memories.

But nothing would end those memories, would it? He could see it all again. That sunny day at the cemetery, staring in grim silence at the two shiny hardwood boxes, all strewn with flowers, suspended over empty, open graves. Oh, the pits were hidden from view by the pretty cloths draped over them. But a kid of fifteen knew well enough what was underneath. A kid of fifteen knew what was inside. A kid knew that all the flowers and pretty words were bull, and that death was the ugliest thing there was.

And he knew he never wanted to hurt like that again. And he wouldn't. He was determined that he wouldn't.

He'd stood, holding his little brother's hand. Elliot had been crying real soft. For days he'd been crying. His nose and eyes were raw from the sting of bitter tears. And it wasn't fair, dammit. It wasn't fair that his little brother had to suffer that way...that any of them had to suffer that way.

Adam ran as the memories spun around in his mind, and he felt the pain and the rage boiling up inside him in a way they never had. He stopped running only when his strength gave out. His body gave up. He fell facedown on the parched, splitting ground and tasted baked dirt on his lips.

And then the storm hit him. A storm he'd never felt, even in the height of his rage. His hands clenched, fingers digging into the sunbaked earth. Teeth bared, eyes tight and burning, he whispered, "Sweet heaven, why? Why the hell did it have to be them? Why did they leave us all alone like that? What right did they have to put a bunch of kids through that kind of heartbreak?"

The tears came...years and years worth of them. The tears of a child mourning the deaths of his mama and his daddy. A child unable to express his grief or his sadness by any means other than rage and anger. The grief, so long held captive, was finally given release.

He sobbed. He had never cried this way in his life. Hell, he hadn't shed a tear since that horrible, black day when his world had fallen apart. Not one tear had fallen. Not one.

But he shed them now.

Why?

Why? The question kept coming back, over and over. Why now? Eventually the storm subsided, but the question remained. It begged his exploration. It demanded his attention. And as he lay there, limp in the aftermath of that emotional onslaught, his mind cleared a bit, and he realized the answer was simple.

He had never loved anyone the way he had loved his parents...not until now. He'd thought he had, but he hadn't, not really. And he had never lost someone who meant as much to him as they had. Not until now.

The storm might have abated, but the pain remained. God, it hurt. He had sworn never to hurt this way again. Yet here it was, swamping him, taking away coherent thought, paralyzing in its power. He wanted to curl into a ball or crawl into a black hole and never emerge. He wanted to drown in the pain until it ended.

Galloping hooves thundered in the distance, drawing nearer. The ground beneath him trembled. He didn't give a damn. The horse pounded up to him, then stopped and snorted and blew and panted while saddle leather creaked and booted feet hit the ground.

"Adam!" A hand fell onto his shoulder. "Adam, are you okay?"

Elliot. His baby brother. The motherless toddler

who had cried for his mama every night for a month. The pudgy-faced angel who had fallen asleep in big brother Garrett's arms only when he was too exhausted to cry anymore. And who had slept half of every night interrupted by the spasming sobs that continued long after his crying stopped. Like echoes...like aftershocks. He didn't even remember, did he? How could he forget that kind of trauma?

His kid brother was a man now. Big, callused hands closed on Adam's shoulders, rolled him over as if he was a featherweight. A man's concerned, narrowed eyes peered down at him from a tanned face.

"What the hell happened?"

Adam shook his head, averted his eyes.

"Talk to me, Adam," Elliot said. Loud and firm, that voice. And for the first time Adam saw a hint of anger in his kid brother's eyes. "I just saw Kirsten at her lawyer's house in broad daylight, bawling like a motherless calf, and I think she was crying even before she found the shock of her life waiting for her there. Now here you are facedown in the dirt and—dammit, Adam, are you crying? What the hell is going on with you two?"

Adam sat up slowly, knuckled his face dry, embarrassed, but still shaking with emotion. Elliot hunkered down low. His anger faded. His touch softened. "Adam?"

When Adam looked at Elliot he saw that chubby-faced toddler crying for his mother. Asking innocently, trustingly, when Daddy was coming home.

The next thing Adam knew, he'd slammed his arms

around his kid brother's shoulders and was holding him hard, speaking muffled words into Elliot's denim shirt. "Dammit, I'm sorry. I'm sorry, El. I didn't know."

Elliot hugged back, slapped Adam's shoulders a few times for good measure, then eased himself free and studied his brother's face worriedly. "Have you been drinking, Adam?"

"I wish to God I had." Adam lowered his head, drew a shaky breath. "It was Kirsten," he managed to say. He levered himself to his feet, slapped at the dirt on his jeans. "Kirsten was driving the car that ran our parents off the road that day, El. It was her."

Elliot stood there a second, blinking. "But...she couldn't have been more than...?"

"Fourteen," Adam filled in. "God, I can't believe...I don't want to believe...but it's true. She told me herself, just this morning."

Elliot closed his eyes briefly. When he opened them again, Adam could see a harsh pain in their depths. "So that's what that Cowan bastard has been holding over her head all this time. The son of a bitch. Whoever shot him deserves the freaking Nobel prize."

Adam shook his head slowly. "*Him?* What about her? She's the one who killed our parents and then spent the next twenty years lying about it."

"Hell, yeah, she lied about it. Wouldn't you? Think about this, Adam—put yourself in her place. You've got yourself a father with a ticker that could give out at any time, and you're in love with the son of the people who died in the accident. What the hell was she supposed to do? She was a kid, for God's sake!"

Adam drew a breath. "She didn't even know at first. Cowan told her they were fine. He sprang the truth on her like a trap on our wedding day, used it to get her to take off with him instead."

Elliot sighed long and low, shaking his head, kicking pebbles. "Can you imagine what that did to her?" he asked. He straightened, took off his hat, kneading the brim as he stared out toward the sunrise. "Finding out on her wedding day that she'd killed her own in-laws?" He kicked a larger rock and sent it sailing. "Man, can you imagine how she must have felt? She had the dress, the flowers, the diamond on her finger. She had to give it all up. All because of that bastard. That vile, soulless bastard who forced her into marrying him when she must have hated his guts. Can you imagine what that must have been like? Living with that creep because of his blackmail? My God, no wonder she's seemed so hard and cold these past two years. She must have had to turn off every feeling she ever had."

Adam had gone still, finally hearing what his brother was saying. He was...he was *sympathizing*...with *Kirsten!* "I can't believe you. You feel *sorry* for her? She killed our parents, Elliot."

"I got that part." Elliot met his eyes, then his brows arched. "Hell, what's wrong with you? You think she did it on purpose? You think it was a premeditated act of malicious violence? It was an *accident,* Adam. She was fourteen years old! You took Dad's car out when you were that age. The same damn thing could just as easily have happened to you!''

Adam swallowed hard. It was true. What Kirsten had done had been an accident. A twenty-year-old accident at that.

''You walked out on her for that, didn't you, Adam? You turned your back on a woman who doesn't have a friend in the world right now, because of a twenty-year-old mistake, a mistake she made when she was no more than a kid.''

''It's more than the mistake!'' Adam shouted back. ''It's the lies. Dammit, Elliot, even if you can forgive the accident, how the hell can you forgive the lies?''

''What *about* those lies, Adam?'' Elliot shook his head, slammed his hat back on. ''You think you wouldn't have done the same thing in her place? You just go ahead and leave that girl in agony. You and your high and mighty morals and your judgmental attitude. You'll be damned lucky if I don't go back there and marry her myself.''

Adam looked up slowly, fists clenching at his sides, a fire rising in his belly so suddenly that he could barely contain it.

''Yeah. I can see in your eyes that you've stopped loving her because of this. Plain as day. Obvious in the way you're looking at me like you want to rip my heart out right now.''

''Elliot…''

''Tell me something, big brother. Would you have lied through your teeth if you thought you could have kept our father alive by doing it?''

The words hit him between the eyes. Hard, and dead-on accurate. Oh, God, Adam thought. He closed his eyes, lowered his head. What the hell had he done?

"Would you, Adam?" Elliot demanded.

Adam lifted his head, met his brother's eyes—wise beyond their years. "You're right. God, you're right. I would," he muttered.

Elliot crossed his arms over his chest and nodded, a smug expression on his face. "I thought so."

Adam looked around for his hat, spotted it, a tiny speck in the distance, and started walking.

"Take the horse," Elliot said. "I brought an extra, or hadn't you noticed?"

Frowning, Adam realized he *hadn't* noticed. He'd been too wrapped up in self-pity and condemnation of the woman he loved to notice much of anything. Elliot had ridden Kirsten's borrowed mount, and he'd apparently been leading Adam's. Adam climbed into the saddle. "Where did you leave Kirsten?"

"I put her at Jessi's place for now. Told her to keep her head down and stay put till I found you and came back. Hell, she was a mess. I doubt she could have gone anywhere even if she'd wanted to."

Adam turned in the saddle. "You said that...she was crying?"

"Crying is a pretty word for what she was doing. And it wasn't pretty, believe me. I never saw a woman in such sorry shape before."

Adam lifted his chin, closed his eyes. He had promised Kirsten that no matter what she confessed to him, he would stand by her. He had vowed he wouldn't run away in anger this time. He had sworn nothing she could have done in the past would make a difference to him. And then he had proceeded to break every pledge he'd made.

"It must have taken one hell of a lot of courage for her to tell you all of that, big brother," Elliot said. "A *hell* of a lot of courage."

Especially since she had so accurately predicted his reaction, Adam thought.

Something was different now. His emotional storm, the one he had just weathered, seemed to have cleansed him somehow. Seemed to have made his vision a little clearer, his head a little sharper. He knew now. It had been an accident, what had happened to his mother and father. They hadn't left of their own accord. It wasn't their fault, and it wasn't Kirsten's....

And it wasn't mine.

And that was the heart of all of this, wasn't it? That was the thing that had been eating at his gut since he was fifteen going on ninety-nine. That the deaths of his parents had somehow been his fault. That he had done something wrong and brought disaster raining down on the family. He was the smartest, the most logical minded, the thinker. And to him, it had seemed impossible that something so tragic could have happened without *some* reason. Some cause. And since he had known deep down that his brothers were too good, that his parents were flawless, that his baby sister was too innocent to have done anything so awful as to bring about this kind of divine retribution, it must have been him. He must have done something. It had to have been his fault.

And he had been living with the guilt of that feeling ever since.

Until now. Kirsten's confession had taken that burden from his shoulders.... And it had given him another target for the blame. He had reacted violently but predictably, lashing out at her and, in the end, abandoning her the way he'd been abandoned by her, and because of her. And then finally, at long last, he had been free to give vent to his grief.

But it wasn't Kirsten's fault, either. And because he knew the pain of living with the idea that something so awful *was* your fault, he had to get back to her. He had to tell her, to make her believe...

Elliot spurred his horse, then leaned sideways in the saddle. Bending so low his head nearly dragged the ground, he scooped up Adam's dropped Stetson in one hand, clung to the pommel with the other and somehow managed to get himself upright again. Then he slowed until Adam caught up to him. Elliot reached up and dropped the hat onto Adam's head.

"Thanks," Adam muttered.

"You're more than welcome."

"Not just for the hat," Adam said.

"I know."

"You've been takin' risks left and right, El."

"I know that, too."

"You seem to show up just when I need you."

"I'm keeping my eye on you, big brother."

Adam swallowed. "Is Wes mad about the horses?"

"You know Wes. He's always mad about something. Taylor smoothed things over, though."

"He can't stay mad when she's around, can he?"

"No chance in hell. Could you?"

Adam almost smiled. "Guess not."

"Jessi and Lash are flying home. Chelsea told them what was going on up here, and Jessi's bound and determined to dive right into the middle of it."

"Like you?"

Elliot shrugged. "She's better at this kind of thing than I am. If Jessi were home, she'd have Kirsten cleared of all charges and the two of you walking down the aisle by now."

Adam lowered his head. "I don't think that's going to happen. I broke every promise I ever made to her...twice now."

"So you just go on back, beg her forgiveness and get busy keeping those promises."

"I wish it were that simple."

Elliot shrugged.

"Then there's the matter of this murder charge," Adam went on.

"Only a heartless slug of a man like Cowan could decide that as long as he was going to die, he might as well take his wife out with him."

Adam lifted a brow. "So you buy that theory?"

"It's the only thing that makes sense. Especially now."

"Now?"

Elliot glanced over at Adam. "That's right, you don't know. I was so damned mad at you for hurting

Kirsten that I forgot to tell you what happened after you left.''

Adam's heart skipped a beat. ''Is she okay?''

''She's in shock, Adam. She made her way over to Stephen Hawkins' place. I was on my way there, too, luckily. Hawkins was supposed to take a copy of Cowan's will over to the rangers' station in El Paso last night. But he never showed. They called him this morning, got no answer, so they asked Garrett to send someone out there, and I volunteered.''

''And?''

Elliot nodded. ''I got there about the time Kirsten let out her first scream. She'd arrived first and found Hawkins hanging from a light fixture over his kitchen table. The suicide note was pinned to his shirt.''

Adam's throat went dry. He grimaced as he realized how horrible it must have been for Kirsten. He should have been there, should have been with her.

''My God,'' he managed.

''Yeah. And I didn't have time to look around a whole lot, but I have a feeling that will is long gone. Garrett's over there now, searching the place for it.''

''Then...you think this is all tied up somehow with Cowan's murder?''

Elliot nodded. ''I sure as hell do.''

Adam's blood seemed to chill and thicken up in his veins. ''And Kirsten's all alone,'' he muttered. Then he kicked the mare's sides, and she lunged into a powerful gallop.

They rode at a dead run the rest of the way back to town, through the streets, across the lawn and right up to Jessi's little cottage. Dismounting, Adam tied his horse, then glanced up and down the road, but he saw no prying eyes, no killers lurking. He moved quickly to the door at the front of the house.

And then his blood ran cold.

The door stood open. Shards of broken glass spiked from its window. Hinges creaked in whispers as the breeze moved the door slightly back and forth.

"Oh, no…"

He pushed the door open cautiously, peered inside. "Kirsten?"

But there was no answer. And he no longer needed one. Jessi's house looked as if a wrestling match had gone on inside.

Kirsten was gone. But it was pretty obvious that she hadn't gone willingly. Someone had come here, while Elliot was away, and they'd taken her. And it looked as if she had put up one hell of a fight.

Adam closed his eyes and cursed himself for having left her this morning. God, if anything happened to her, he would never forgive himself.

Chapter 12

He'd been searching Jessi's house—seeking some kind of clue as to who had been here and where they'd taken Kirsten—for only a few minutes when a hand fell heavily on Adam's shoulder from behind. He whirled, adrenaline surging, fist coming up automatically, ready to nail whoever dared mess with him at a time like this and immediately thinking of the killer.

Garrett stood there, eyed the fist that had frozen halfway to his face and shook his head slowly. "I let you get away with that once, Adam. But I wouldn't be pushing my luck if I were you. I don't have much patience for kid brothers with violent tendencies."

Adam lowered his hand and his head, his breath rushing out of him all at once. "I'm sorry. God, I'm sorry, Garrett. About hitting you before. I had to get Kirsten the hell out of there. I couldn't let her go to

jail any more than you could stand by and let someone
lock Chelsea up in a cell when you knew damned good
and well she was innocent.''

"Or even if I thought she might not be,'' Garrett
said. Then he eyed Adam with a frown. "You felt that
strongly about it, huh?'' he asked, searching his
brother's face.

"Yeah. I did.''

"So that's it. I kinda figured.''

Adam shook his head. "I never should have hit you
like that—''

"Yeah, and I never should have gone down so easy.
Just figured it was for the best. I sure as hell didn't
want to hit you back, and if I'd gotten up again, you
would have forced me to.''

Adam lowered his head. "So Elliot was right. You
took the fall and let us go.''

"Hey, don't look so disappointed. You pack a mean
punch. Just not quite as mean as my jawbone.'' Garrett
rubbed the spot. "Besides, it *did* leave a bruise.'' Then
he stopped kidding and looked around the room.
"What happened here?''

"Elliot didn't tell you on the phone when he called
to tell you to get over here?''

Elliot appeared from another room. He and Adam
had been searching the house for clues, but so far,
they'd found nothing. "Hell, no, I didn't tell him on
the phone,'' he said. "I didn't know who might be
with him. God knows half the El Paso rangers were
over at Hawkins' place with him earlier. I sure didn't
want them all showing up here!'' He shook his head.

"Well, I'm here, and I'm alone, so you can tell me now. What the hell happened?"

"Someone broke in and took Kirsten," Elliot announced. "And we're afraid it's the same guy who murdered Joseph Cowan."

"Garrett, we have to find her," Adam said, and he could hear the desperation in his own voice…but he didn't care. "The son of a bitch took a shot at the border patrol last night and damn near started a war. She could have been killed, Garrett, and I think that's exactly what this guy wants. He wants her dead." Adam paced away, pushing a hand through his hair. "I know we didn't part on the best of terms, but I need your help. Kirsten needs your help. And it wasn't her fault, what I did—"

"Can it, Adam. You're my brother. You know I'll do whatever I can."

"I'm running outside the law here, Garrett," Adam said, a warning tone to his voice.

"The hell with the law. This is blood."

Adam met Garrett's eyes, saw the bond they shared reflected there, and nodded once.

Garrett turned to Elliot. "Did you find anything here?"

"Nothing."

Shaking his head, Garrett looked around. "You say you think this clown wants her dead. But if that's the case, Adam, why didn't he just kill her right here? Why drag her off someplace else?"

Adam blew air through clenched teeth. "I don't know. Hell, maybe he wants to make it look like an accident or a sui—'' There he stopped, his head coming up slowly. ''Or a suicide.''

''Just like Stephen Hawkins, maybe,'' Elliot interjected. When both men swung their stunned gazes his way, he went on. ''Hell, boys, I don't know about you, but it sure seems strange to me that old boy got a hankering to hang himself right in the middle of all of this.''

''But he left a note,'' Adam said, recalling Elliot's earlier reporting of the event. ''You said he left a note.'' Elliot nodded, looking at Garrett.

Garrett nodded. ''Yeah, there was a note, all right. A very *brief* note. 'A gentleman knows not to linger too long at the dance' was all it said. It was in his handwriting. But sloppy as hell. Like he was good and drunk when he wrote it…or something.''

''I'd bet on the 'or something,''' Elliot muttered. ''Hawkins didn't drink.''

''When will we get some autopsy results to tell us for sure?'' Adam asked.

''Not as soon as we need 'em. But I might be able to get a blood alcohol on him by now. The pathologist is an old friend. He's had Hawkins for over an hour now, and I asked him to run a few tests of his own, so we won't have to wait for the results on the samples sent to the state crime lab. Won't be admissible in court, but at least we'll know.'' Garrett headed for Jessi's telephone, then seemed to think better of it and went outside instead. Adam and Elliot followed.

Sliding into the front seat of his pickup, leaving the door open, Garrett yanked up his mobile phone and tapped in a number. A second later he was speaking. "Sheriff Brand here. Get me Doc Leighy." There was a pause, then, "John, it's Garrett. Got anything for me?" He nodded at the phone, waited a moment, then lifted his brows. "Just what *is* that, John? Sleeping pills?" Pause. "Um-hmm. I see. Okay." Another pause. "My brother?" And his eyes met Adam's. "Nope, no sign of him. He takes off like this when he gets upset, sometimes. Tell your friend the ranger I said he'll turn up soon enough. And that no, I have no reason to suspect he's anywhere near Kirsten Armstrong. They hate each other's guts, you know."

Garrett replaced the receiver, sent Adam a level, serious look.

"Thanks," Adam said.

"*De nada.* They didn't find alcohol in Hawkins' blood, but they did find large amounts of a tranquilizer commonly used in over-the-counter sleeping pills."

Adam blinked. "Sleeping pills? Does that make Hawkins' death a murder, as well?"

Garrett shook his head. "Not necessarily. Pretty common for a suicide to take piles of sleeping pills and either vomit them up or decide they aren't working fast enough and then move on to another method. The rangers are working on that assumption."

"You agree with them?"

"No."

"Neither do I," Elliot said softly. He looked at Garrett. "Did you find Joe Cowan's will in any of Stephen Hawkins' files?"

Garrett shook his head. "No. We turned the place upside down, but there was no sign of it."

"I didn't think there would be," Elliot said. "And isn't it odd how reluctant Hawkins seemed to be to turn it over? First he tells the rangers he doesn't remember what was in it, then he says he'll pull the file and send it over, then he stalls and delays, and finally he kills himself, and the will is still nowhere to be found."

"You think the killer took it?" Adam asked.

"Either that, or Hawkins hid it himself. The question is, why would he do that?"

Adam racked his brain, but found no answer there. He glanced at Garrett. "What do you think?"

"Well, I don't think Hawkins' death was a suicide, boys. And if that proves to be the case, then it makes sense to assume that anything missing from his home was taken by whoever killed him."

Adam nodded toward Jessi's trashed house. "I noticed you didn't tell the rangers about the break-in and Kirsten being abducted."

"No, I didn't," Garrett said. "I suppose there's a chance they could help us track Kirsten down, but they'd haul her off to jail the second they found her. I'm thinking we can do just as well on our own. Maybe better. As soon as you took off with Kirsten, Adam, I realized that this...this was a family thing."

"Family," Adam repeated, not sure he understood what his brother was getting at.

"You love her, don't you?"

Adam lowered his head quickly, avoiding Garrett's eyes, but doubting that it did much good.

"He loves her," Elliot said.

"He'd damn well better love her," Garrett went on. "I'd hate to think he coldcocked his favorite brother for anything less."

Adam sighed, shaking his head. He didn't know what he felt for Kirsten right now. He just knew he wanted her back, alive, safe…so he could find out.

"So in my book," Garrett went on, "that makes her family." Garrett slapped Adam's shoulder. "So the family's involved now."

Adam blinked, looking from Elliot to Garrett and back again. The two exchanged knowing looks. "What do you mean, the family's involved?"

Garrett shrugged. "You know how it goes with this crew. So damned close knit that when one Brand gets kicked, another one yips. And it's sheer hell to keep a secret in this family."

Elliot nodded. "Jessi and Lash will be arriving any time now. They cut their trip short the second Chelsea called to tell them what was going on. The minute they get here, we'll have Jessi take a look around. Well, once she gets done screaming about the mess in her house, that is. If there's a sign which way that son of a bitch took Kirsten and by what means, you know Jessi will spot it."

Garrett picked up there. "Wes is already canvassing town, and if anybody knows a thing, you know they're gonna tell him. Wes scares people. If that isn't enough to make 'em talk, then Taylor will charm the information out of them.''

"Ben and Penny are over at Stephen Hawkins' place," Elliot said. That earned him a glare from Garrett, but he only shrugged sheepishly. "I know, it's a crime scene. But we couldn't wait. Not when Penny and I already came to the conclusion that the lawyer's death has to be involved in all this somehow. And Cowan's missing will seemed fishy to her, too, right from the start. So Penny and Ben are searching Hawkins' house, office and even his car for any files he has on Cowan.''

"Waste of time," Garrett said. "I told you, Elliot, the rangers and I went through that place with a finetooth comb. For God's sake, they only cleared out of there within the last half hour.''

"Yeah, well, Nancy Drew they ain't," Elliot drawled.

"Neither is Penny," Garrett retorted.

"Don't let her hear you say that," Elliot said, grinning.

Garrett rolled his eyes. "Great. I wonder who's gonna be sheriff when I get run out of town on a rail?" But then he lifted his head and continued. "Out at the ranch, Chelsea's got a list of Cowan's household employees, and she's tracking them down by phone. Said she couldn't sit still and do nothing. Sara's out there helping her. She came up from El Paso as soon as she heard what was going on. Marcus and Casey stayed there. They're working through that computer network

Marcus's old friend Graham uses. Checking out business contacts of Cowan's and so on.''

''Hell. Sounds like we've got every Brand in Texas
working on this thing,'' Adam said slowly. He was
touched. Not surprised, but moved beyond words. No
wonder he'd been so miserable in New York. He'd
been away from this damned bunch of meddling pains
in the backside. Too far away. And he'd missed them.

''You got that right,'' Elliot interjected. ''And if
that isn't enough, we can always call in the Oklahoma
branch of the family. Though I hesitate to get that
rowdy bunch involved in anything this volatile.'' He
sent Adam a wink.

Adam wished he could feel as upbeat as Elliot
sounded. But he didn't. He was scared, damned
scared. ''None of that's gonna do a bit of good if this
guy—whoever he is—has already killed her,'' he said
slowly. He paced away from the pickup, stared off
down the road. ''I never should have stormed out on
her the way I did. I just... When she told me what
she'd done, I just...''

Garrett looked at him. ''I guess I'm missing something here.''

Adam and Elliot exchanged glances. Elliot put a
hand on Garrett's arm. ''It's not the time for that now,
Garrett. But we do have to talk. All of us, the whole
clan. But later. After Kirsten is safe and sound.''

Garrett eyed him, then Adam.

''No,'' Adam said. ''If he's going to be risking his
badge to help her, he has to know about this first. It's
only right, Elliot.''

"Know about what?" Garrett demanded.

"Fine," Elliot said. "But we're wasting time standing here. Let's head over to the Cowan mansion and go from there. And on the way, Garrett, Adam and I will tell you about Kirsten's revelations."

"No one is ever going to believe I killed myself," Kirsten said slowly. She watched Phillip's eyes. And what she saw there shook her. Madness. Sickness. There was something just not right about those eyes. And she had a feeling that reasoning with the man wasn't going to work. He was beyond reason. But she had to try. "This isn't going to work."

"Of course they'll believe it. Now, come on, swallow the tablet like a good girl." He pressed the barrel of the gun harder against her temple, thumbed the hammer back. The sound of it was like a jolt to her nervous system. God, if his finger slipped, if he even moved wrong...

"Okay, okay, just move that damned thing away from my head."

The barrel stayed put. Thick, salty fingertips pushed a capsule between her lips, and she felt the urge to rinse her mouth out with soap. Then a glass was put in their place, and she sipped the water, but didn't swallow the pill. She moved it underneath her tongue. It began to dissolve there, its bitter taste coating her mouth, but she managed not to grimace, and she forced herself not to swallow it.

The glass moved away fast. "Now open up, and let me see."

Obediently, Kirsten opened her mouth. He leaned close, looking inside, then thrust his big fingers in, to check under her tongue. She bit him. It was the only thing she could think of to do.

Phillip leapt backward, yelping in pain. "Damn you!" he cried.

"Damn *you!*" she said. "You're the one going around killing people, not me."

"I'm going to be a millionaire, though," he said. "And you're just going to be a dead woman. Hell, I'd rather be the killer than the victim any day." He smiled slowly. "And I'd far rather be the millionaire than the lowly driver and devoted sidekick. Wouldn't you?"

"Well, you aren't going to be either one, Phillip. The only thing you're going to be is a prisoner of the state of Texas."

The pill. The pill was gone. Thoroughly dissolved in her mouth now. Gooey slime lingered, coating her tongue and the roof of her mouth. She wanted to spit, but if she did, he would see. She couldn't even bring a hand to her mouth, because they were tied to the sides of the chair, and her ankles were bound to the legs of it, as they had been since he'd brought her here.

They were in Phillip's apartment. The spacious apartment above the large garage at the estate. The detested mansion was right next door. But no one was there. No one would know she was anywhere near this place. No one would have any reason to think she might be, or to look for her here.

Phillip jammed another pill into her mouth, shoved the water glass to her lips so hard its rim hit her teeth, and tipped it up. She pressed her lips against the water that flowed. Icy cold, it ran down her chin, soaked the front of her blouse, chilled her tension-warmed skin. She shivered in reaction to the cold and the fear.

Phillip pinched her nose, swearing at her. "Open. Open, dammit!"

Kirsten twisted, writhed, and her lungs pulled against her sealed airways, starving, screaming, until she had to open her mouth for air. When she did, Phillip poured water into her mouth instead. Water she inhaled and choked and gagged on. Gasping, panting, coughing, she tried to speak, but the words were hoarse and raspy.

"You nearly drowned me!"

"I'm going to do far worse to you if you don't cooperate and do what you're told." He checked her mouth. The pill was gone. She supposed she must have swallowed it, despite her best efforts not to.

She leaned back in the chair, head tipped back, eyes focused on the ceiling. "You're really going to kill me, aren't you?"

He glanced at her briefly, and when their eyes locked, she thought she saw something flash in his— some spark of remorse—but it was so brief she couldn't even be certain it was real.

"I don't have any choice," he said, looking away, sullen, eyes downcast.

"Will you...will you at least tell me why? I've always been kind to you, haven't I, Phillip? I never did anything to hurt you...."

"That's got nothing to do with it." His back was toward her now. He paced. She was shaking him up, just a bit, with her questions. Good. She would keep going, then. Shake him up as much as she could.

"I just don't see why you think killing me will make you a millionaire," she said.

"You don't see anything, do you, Kirsten? You're blind."

She drew a breath, slow, deep. "I...I could, though. If you let me live, I could make you a millionaire. I don't want Joseph's money. I hated the man, you know that. I could give it all to you. All of it. I'd sign it over right now."

He stopped pacing and turned to face her, eyes narrow. "And you'd take me to court later, claiming I'd forced you. No. Joseph cared for me. *I* was loyal to him. *I* took care of him. And unlike you, you ungrateful, faithless bitch, *I* always did what he wanted. And *this*, Kirsten Cowan, is *exactly* what he wanted."

Fear clutched her heart. The phone started shrilling again, but he ignored it as he'd done every time it had rung before. He reached for another capsule. Distract him, she thought.

"You killed him. How can you claim to have loved Joseph when you killed him?"

Phillip went still for a moment. His eyes closed tight. "He was suffering so much...the medication...hell, it wasn't strong enough. He didn't care. He only wanted to live long enough to have an heir, anyway, but *you* denied him that. Denied a dying man's last wish! Deceived him!'' Phillip shook his head slowly.

''Then...he knew?''

''About your secret little stash of birth control pills? Yeah. He knew. That was when he planned all this, Kirsten, right after he found out about those pills. That was the one thing you did that he couldn't forgive, and he decided then and there to make you pay.''

Lifting her chin, she faced him. ''I knew it,'' she whispered. ''I knew he was somehow pulling the strings, making all this happen to me.''

Phillip smiled a sick, twisted smile. ''Oh, yeah. He was too smart for you. He's been playing you like a fiddle, Kirsten, and you've been dancing in time. You thought you could beat him. Even the cancer thought it could beat him. But he won in the end. He cheated the cancer. Wouldn't let it kill him. No, not Joseph. He died on his own terms and arranged things so that you'd pay for your betrayal, as well.''

''And so you'd be rewarded for your loyalty? Is that how it is?''

Phillip nodded, leaned closer. ''That's how it is. He arranged it so I would get everything. All I have to do is make sure you're out of the way first.''

He gripped her chin in one hand and stuffed another pill into her mouth. This time he crammed his hand so far into her throat that the capsule went partway down dry. Then he clamped her chin hard, to force her mouth to stay closed, and he held her nose. She had to swallow if she wanted to breathe again. Her head began to swim. From lack of oxygen or the sleeping pills. She wasn't certain which. Maybe both.

She swallowed the pill to avoid choking or suffocation.

He let go, and Kirsten sucked in huge gulps of air, letting her head fall back against the wooden chair. The ceiling was spinning now.

Phillip smiled. "Time to write the suicide note, Kirsten."

"I won't," she managed to croak. "You can't make me do this."

He laughed a little. Opened a drawer. Pulled out an odd-looking device and thumbed a button. A crackling sound, a flash and sparks. "Stun gun," he said. "It won't leave any marks. And believe me, you'll do what I tell you."

She eyed the thing in his hand. And she wished to God Adam had kept his word not to turn his back on her this time. But more than that. She wished she'd told him how much she loved him. And how she had never stopped. Not in all this time. She wished she could see him just once more before her husband's insane driver took her life. But wishes were pretty much useless to her now.

The only chance she had left was to stall for time and pray someone would come looking for her. Even the Texas Rangers. Anyone.

Stalling for time, however, was going to cost her. It was going to cost her dearly.

Phillip held the stun gun close to her skin and let it

crackle and spark. "You ready to write the note, Kirsten?" he asked her, the thing poised and ready.

She lifted her head, called up her resolve, met his eyes and said firmly, "No."

Chapter 13

Of all of Cowan's employees, the only one Chelsea Brand had been unable to contact was Phillip Carr, the driver. A driver named Carr. She should have known right away something was wrong with that. The address she had for him was the same as the estate, so he must have an apartment out there.

"Sara?" she called.

Her young cousin by marriage popped into the kitchen at once, holding little Bubba's chubby hand in hers. A schoolteacher, Sara was terrific with kids of any age. "Yeah, Chelsea?"

"Would you stay with Bubba while I run an errand?"

Sara nodded, but she looked a little worried. Still, she knew better than to argue. "Sure" was all she said.

Chelsea nodded, grabbed her keys and headed out. She was going out to that Cowan estate herself, and she wasn't coming back until she had some answers.

"Tell me what you know or I'll damn well beat it out of you!" Wes grabbed the bartender by the lapels and shook him.

The man shook his head fast. "I thought you'd turned peaceable, Wes! Didn't I hear you were some kinda medicine man or—"

"Yeah. One with a temper. Now talk!"

"Honey, maybe if we just asked nicely?" Taylor suggested, easing the frightened man from Wes's grip, smoothing his shirt down, smiling up at him with huge dark eyes. "It *is* asking a lot."

"Dern right it is," the bartender said. "Cowan's dead, Hawkins is dead, and now young Kirsten's gone missing. I could be next."

"You're damn straight you could," Wes growled. "Might be sooner than you think."

The guy swallowed with a loud gulping sound. "Okay, but you didn't hear this from me. That driver of Cowan's...Carr's his name...well, Nora—you know Nora? My best waitress?"

"I know her."

"Her boy Joey works over at the drugstore part-time, and he told her that Carr came in the other day and bought himself three bottles of sleepin' pills. Now, I thought that was kinda odd. Don't you?"

"Where's this Carr live?"

"Out at the Cowan estate, far as I know."

Wes nodded once, turned to his wife. "Stay here."

"Yeah," she said. "Right. You know darn well I'm gonna do just that, hon."

He scowled at her. She smiled at him. "That legendary temper of yours doesn't scare me one bit, Wes."

His scowl died. "Never did. Stay beside me, then, okay? There could be trouble."

She nodded and stayed close beside him as they headed out the door.

Jessi handed Lash the baby as she scanned the mess inside her house. Her eyes wide and round, she cussed a blue streak, then turned and walked right back outside again. "Something's happened here. And ten to one it all has to do with my brother Adam and the woman he never should have let get away. Dang, Lash, come out here and look at this!"

Lash followed, with little Maria Michele snuggling happily in his arms. He looked down at the ground. Saw grass. Dirt. A couple of stones. And knew darned well his wife saw far more.

"Someone was dragged outta here kicking and screaming. A woman." Jessi thrust a forefinger toward the ground. "Small feet."

"Obviously," Lash said, still seeing nothing. He wondered if his gun was still in the house, or if the intruder had stolen it, whoever he was. He didn't even think to doubt his wife's words about what she saw in that ordinary-looking patch of lawn and sidewalk.

He hurried inside, located his gun and badge safe

and sound in the closet, took them out and headed back outside, baby still bouncing merrily on his hip, wearing her Mickey Mouse ears tall and proudly on her head.

By now Jessi was hunkered down, examining the road. Lash trotted to catch up. When he reached her, she was squatting over a set of tire tracks that he could at least see.

"He pulled, dragged or carried her this far. The car was here." Her fingers touched the marks on the road. "Shoot, honey, he was driving a limo."

"But nobody around here has a limo...except Cowan, and he's—" With a glance at his daughter, Lash censored himself.

"We'd better get over there," Jessi said. "We'll drop Maria Michele at Mrs. Plunkwell's on the way." She glanced at the gun he carried. "Did you bring one for me?"

Great, Lash thought. It was going to be another shoot-out, another one of those insane episodes that were only supposed to happen in old movies and Louis L'Amour novels. He'd married into the most trouble-prone bunch of Texans in the entire Lone Star state.

"Never mind," Jessi said. "I'll go get it." She ruffled the baby's hair and hurried back to the house for her cannon—with which she was fully capable of shooting the eye out of a mosquito at fifty yards.

Hell of a woman. Hell of a family. Lash didn't regret getting involved with either of them.

The baby cooed. Lash looked over to see Mrs.

Plunkwell standing on her lawn, watching him. He waved, she waved back and he carried the baby over.

Penny Lane Brand was one hell of a private eye, even at six months pregnant. But when there was nothing to find, there was nothing to find. And Ben could feel her disappointment coming at him in waves.

They'd searched Stephen Hawkins' house, his office, his car, his attic, even his back lawn and basement. They'd turned over cushions, lifted up carpets, checked above the ceiling panels and in the soil of the houseplants. Nothing. No sign of Cowan's will.

Time to move on, time to think of some other way to help Penny's best friend, Kirsten.

Ben slipped his arm around Penny's shoulders and squeezed. "We'll come up with something, hon. I know we will."

"I know," she said. "But will it be in time? This is frustrating! Why wouldn't Hawkins have that will here? It's like he hid it deliberately."

Ben shook his head. "Garrett thinks the killer took it."

"No." Penny paced, head down, deep in thought. "No. And that's just what's bugging me about this. If the killer had taken the will, there would still be something here. The rest of Cowan's file. An empty folder. Another copy. A file on the computer. There's nothing. Nothing, Ben."

"And you think that means…?" he prompted, then awaited a reply. She was thinking something. She was always thinking something.

"What if Hawkins hid it himself?"

"Why would he?"

Penny shrugged. "Won't know that until we find it. The police wanted it to use as evidence against Kirsten. The will would have given her a motive...so what if Hawkins hid it to buy Kirsten some more time? What if he was trying to help her?"

She paced some more, thought some more. "Or maybe he wasn't hiding it from the police. Maybe he was hiding it from the killer for some reason."

Ben shrugged. "Like you said, when we find it, we'll probably know. That will must hold all the answers." He opened Hawkins' front door, and the two of them stepped out and walked toward Ben's truck. A small white bulldog stood in the front seat, forepaws on the window glass, staring out at them. Olive went just about everywhere they did. Her pups might rule the roost at home, but Olive was queen of the pickup truck.

Ben stopped walking when a small car with a U.S. Mail emblem on it slowed down, veered over, then stopped right in front of Stephen Hawkins' old-fashioned rural mailbox. An arm emerged from the car window, dumping a manila envelope into the mailbox. Then the car moved away.

Ben and Penny looked at each other. Penny smiled. "Of course," she whispered. "That's it, Ben."

Ben ran to the mailbox, yanked the envelope out and stared at the label. The "from" address was the same as the "to." "He mailed it to himself?" Ben asked.

"I should have figured. Best way in the world to buy time. A couple of days, at least. No one's gonna find something once it's in the mail. Not until it gets where it's going, at least." Penny took the envelope from him and ripped it open. She pulled the last will and testament of Joseph Cowan out of its envelope and began flipping pages, her eyes moving rapidly over line upon line of text. Until finally she sighed and shook her head slowly.

"My God, that man was evil."

"What is it, Penny?" Ben asked, moving closer.

She looked up, meeting her husband's eyes. "He left everything to Kirsten with the provision that should anything happen to her before his wishes could be carried out, then everything would go instead to one Phillip Carr." She lifted her head. "He might as well have paid Carr to kill her. So long as it doesn't look like a murder, and it's done before she inherits, he gets everything."

"But then, if this Carr was supposed to kill Kirsten anyway, why bother making it look like she'd killed Cowan?"

"I don't know," Penny said. "To make sure she'd never get a thing, even if Carr failed? To stall her getting her inheritance long enough for him to have the chance to kill her? To make sure Carr wouldn't end up taking the rap for Cowan's murder himself, allowing Kirsten to go free and inherit the money? Maybe all of the above," Penny said. "Who the hell is this guy, anyway? Phillip Carr...why does that name sound so familiar?"

"Carr," Ben repeated. "Wait a minute, isn't that the name of Cowan's driver? Yeah, that's right," he said with barely a pause, answering his own question. "I always thought it was strange that he had a driver named Carr. Doesn't he live—"

"At the estate. Come on!" Penny grabbed her husband's hand, clutching the will in her other one, and raced to the truck.

The Brands gathered beyond the gates of the Cowan estate, a few at a time. Adam, Garrett and Elliot had been the first to arrive. They'd stopped when they'd seen the limo parked in front of the garage. It hadn't been there before. So they left the pickup a safe distance away, out of sight, and then crouched in the bushes, whispering their plan of attack.

Chelsea arrived on their heels. They hadn't heard her pull up, because she'd left her car near where they'd left the truck, and walked in the rest of the way.

"It's gotta be that Phillip Carr," she whispered, crouching beside them.

Adam was so startled he damn near fell over.

"She's right," Penny said.

Adam swung his head around to see Penny and Ben creeping nearer, and, behind them, Wes and Taylor bringing up the rear. "How did you all know we were here?" he asked.

"We didn't," Ben said. "We came looking for Carr. We found the will, Adam, and it's set up so that if something happens to Kirsten, Carr inherits the works."

Wes nodded. "So that's why. I figured it was him when I found out he'd been stockpiling sleeping pills. So what's the game plan?"

"He's got Kirsten in there," Adam said slowly. He looked at his family members, one by one.

"Then let's go in and get her out!" Jessi said.

"No, wait. There's something you need to know first." Adam licked his lips, swallowed hard. "Jessi, Wes, Ben...Kirsten told me why she married Cowan in the first place. And it's...it's liable to change your minds about her, once you know the truth."

"He was holding something over her," Ben said. "She confided that much to me a long time ago, but she would never say what."

Adam nodded. "She told me. And I have to tell you. It's...about the accident that killed our parents...."

Ben, Jessi and Wes exchanged stunned looks. But they all stayed silent and listened intently while Adam spoke. He told them everything Kirsten had told him. He told them his reaction. And he told them that he wouldn't blame them if they wanted to walk away from this rescue now that they knew the truth.

No one said a word for a long moment, and it was Jessi who finally spoke up. "Do you think our mama would have held any of this against Kirsten?"

"No," Ben said softly. "And our daddy wouldn't have turned his back on a girl in trouble, either. She was a kid, Adam. She was a kid."

Adam nodded and met Wes's eyes. "What about you?"

Wes drew a slow breath. "I'm resisting the urge to knock you on your backside, Adam. For walking out on her."

"Amen to that," Jessi said.

"What are we waiting for?" Garrett asked finally. "That girl in there is family."

Jessi lifted her brows and looked from Garrett to Adam. "Is she?"

"Yeah," Adam said. "Yeah, she is."

"Hot damn," Jessi said. "Then let's get our butts in there and get her out."

Everyone spoke in agreement. Adam choked back tears. "Thanks, you guys."

"Enough, already," Wes said. "What's the plan?"

Kirsten's hand moved a half beat behind Phillip's commands. His harshly spoken words seemed to go directly from his lips to the pen in her hand, without bothering to make a pit stop at her brain. She didn't know what she scrawled across the page, or even if it would be legible when she finished. She didn't care. Her body was still shuddering with residual electricity. Tremors worked up her spine and slammed into the base of her skull every once in a while. The discomfort had eased up a whole lot, though, once those sleeping pills had decided to kick in full force. Their effect was numbing. And she was grateful for it at this point.

Her head felt like lead. Her limbs heavy, the pen like a log in her hand.

"Sign it."

She blinked up at Phillip, then shook herself and

stared down at the uneven words dancing drunkenly across the page. Her vision was none too clear. "I killed my husband and find I can't live without him. The guilt of what I have done is driving me insane. There's only one way out. One way to atone. And that is by following my Joseph to the grave."

Narrowing her eyes on the sloppy words, she felt her lips pull into a grimace. "I wouldn't follow that bastard inside if it were raining out." But her words sounded funny. The vowels slurred, and the consonants didn't make the trip to her ears or feel as if they were happening on her lips. Her *s*-words were lisped, as if she had gaps in her teeth.

"Sign it, Kirsten."

She threw the pen down on the table.

Phillip picked up his stun gun and flicked the switch, and Kirsten cried out automatically, flinching back into her chair so hard it tipped over. She crashed to the floor and lay there, closing her eyes, wishing for a miracle.

Phillip didn't pick her up. He came closer, leaned over her with the crackling little torture device, and her eyes flew open when she heard it. The ropes binding her upper arms and waist to the back of the chair pulled tighter as she tried to move away. They cut into her ankles as she pulled against them. He leaned closer, closer, the nose of that horrible device hovering a hairbreadth from her shoulder. Tears streamed, and sobs wrenched at her sternum. "P-please...I'll sign it. J-just give me the pen."

Smiling, Phillip backed off. He gave the chair a

kick, so it tipped to the side. Then he knelt, shoving the paper onto the floor near her hand, sticking the pen between her thumb and forefinger. Barely able to see through her tears, she scratched her name onto the bottom of the sheet. Phillip yanked the paper away so fast she barely saw it move.

He turned away from her. The pen was still in her hand. Kirsten maneuvered it into her sleeve, pushing it up farther and farther until it was out of sight. Then she thought it might not have mattered. He was paying very little attention to her now. Instead, he was pacing. Pacing, with the note in his hand, reading it over, and thinking.

Of how he would kill her, she supposed.

Then he stopped. "More pills would be simplest, of course, but it would take too long. They'll be looking for you soon." Again he began pacing. "And they can't find you here."

Then suddenly he came to where she and the chair lay toppled on the floor, reached down and yanked her upright. The tugging hurt her arm, but she was beyond caring about that. Phillip crouched behind her to untie the ropes. "The house," he told her. "The very room where Joseph died. Using the same gun would be nice. Dramatic, you know? But of course, the police have that. Still, this will be almost as good. We'll make it…poetic."

He freed the ropes from around her ankles, jerked her to her feet and pulled her with him to the door. She staggered, feet feeling oversized and clumsy as the blood rushed back into them. They prickled and stung. She tripped. And still he kept her moving through the door and toward the outside stairway. Frantically, she searched the driveway. Why wasn't anyone coming for her?

Because she had no one. No one who cared, anyway. Adam hated her, and if he'd told his family what she'd done, then they all must feel the same by now. Even big, sweet Ben. Even Penny, who'd been her best friend. Odd that she'd once thought of them, all of them, as the next best thing to her own family. Odd that she'd kept that feeling alive all this time, even though she'd been estranged from them.

This time it would be permanent.

"You know, in some primitive cultures it was common to send a man's wife to the grave with him. I don't imagine *they* always went without…assistance, either." Phillip grinned at her, and she knew he was insane. But not with any true mental illness. Just with greed. A greed she still didn't understand.

Surrounding his second-floor garage apartment was a catwalk. A narrow redwood deck that bordered Phillip's living quarters on all four sides. It was connected to an outside staircase that led to the ground. There were indoor stairs, as well, so he could go directly from his apartment to the spacious four-car garage below if need be.

They stood now on the catwalk, Kirsten clinging to the rail and battling dizziness, Phillip clinging to Kirsten.

And all of a sudden a voice came from below.

"You'd best stop right where you are, Carr. And let the lady go."

Phillip clenched her tighter, reflexively pulling her flush to his chest like a shield as he searched for the owner of that voice.

"Adam?" Kirsten cried. "Adam! Be careful, Adam, he has a gun!" She tried to see him on the ground below but barely caught a glimpse of his strong body before Phillip tugged her away from the railing.

His hand clapped over her mouth, silencing her. He pressed his back to the wall and eased toward the door. But when he did it was flung open, and Wes Brand stood there looking dark and menacing. He'd come up from the garage, Kirsten realized.

"Do what my brother says, pal," Wes said softly. He had a bowie knife in his hand and a steely glint in his eyes. "Let her go."

Phillip jerked backward, tugging her around a corner. The outside stairs came into view. But at the bottom of them stood another Brand. Big, blond Ben, coming slowly upward.

Trapped. Phillip had to let her go now. There was no way out for him. He was trapped.

Or was he?

Phillip pulled her with him again, rounding another corner. She glimpsed more people on the ground. Lash and Jessi and Penny. And before anyone could guess what Phillip was going to do, he yanked open a window and dived back inside, carrying her with him. They hit the floor hard and rolled. She heard Garrett's voice from outside shouting, "They're back in the apartment!" She heard the door crash open as someone, probably Wes, charged inside. But Phillip was already springing to his feet, tugging her through a door, locking it behind him and then hauling her up a steep, dark set of stairs that led to the A-shaped attic above the apartment.

Dust. Cobwebs. Utter darkness. They might have thought to place men in the garage below, on the ground and on the stairs, but the Brands would not have thought of this.

Phillip hauled her through the trapdoor at the top of the attic stairs, then slammed the trapdoor down. He tugged her farther. Moving backward across the attic all the way to the far wall, watching that trapdoor all the way.

His back reached the far wall, and Kirsten glimpsed the last set of rickety steps, these so steep they seemed more like a ladder than a stairway. They had to lead to the roof. There was nowhere else to go. And then she realized…they went to the widow's walk, at the very peak. Her knees went weak at the thought of the height.

At that same moment the trapdoor rose upward.

Adam's head poked through.

"Oh, God, Adam…" It was so good just to see his face. She felt it had been forever, when in fact it had been only a couple of hours since he'd left her. She was weak, dizzy, hurting, and yet overwhelmed at this chance to look into his blue eyes once more.

"Are you okay?" Adam asked her.

She nodded. "Adam, I—"

"Shut up!" Phillip's gun pressed hard to Kirsten's sternum, right between her breasts, barrel slanted upward. If he squeezed the trigger just then, she thought, terrified, the bullet would rip an inclining path of hell from her chest to her throat and probably exit through the back of her head. She wouldn't stand a chance.

"You just get back down there," Phillip said to Adam. "You just go, or I'll have to kill her."

"Now, you know I can't do that." Adam came very slowly up, holding up both hands, making no threatening gestures. "I'm unarmed, see?"

"I don't give a damn! Get out or I'll kill her now. Is that what you want?"

"Now, what good is that gonna do you, Phillip? Hmm? It won't get you Cowan's fortune. Not with so many witnesses here to testify that it was murder."

"I don't care. I don't care! And you shouldn't either, Brand. Don't you know what she did? Don't you know she's the one who killed your parents? I was there, I saw it!"

"I know. I know. But that was an accident." He took a step closer. "She was a kid. And it was a long time ago, Phil."

"If I were you, I'd want her to die for that. I'd want her to pay."

"Oh, she's paid." Adam found Kirsten's eyes, held them with his. "She's paid in spades for something that was never her fault to begin with."

She blinked as pain rose up to engulf her.

"You...you can forgive her for what she did?"

"Of course I can," Adam said, still holding her eyes, his own gleaming. "See, I've got no choice there, Phillip. I love her. Always have."

Kirsten's knees buckled. She slid downward, but Phillip yanked her upright again. Tears flooded her eyes, and she parted her lips to speak, to tell Adam how much she loved him, how sorry she was. But no sound came from her lips. She couldn't even feel them. The pills. The electrocution. She wasn't even going to be conscious for much longer. She couldn't speak. But she clung to Adam with her eyes and prayed he could see her feelings in them. She tried to mouth the words *I love you. I'm sorry.*

He nodded almost imperceptibly, sending her the same unspoken message in return. "Listen, Carr—" Adam began.

"Don't call me that!"

Adam went silent. Kirsten tried to fight her way through the fog in her brain to understanding. "B-but it's your name," she whispered, surprised to hear the rasp come from her lips. A moment ago she'd tried to speak and had been unable to. Now words were coming out without her permission.

"It's *not* my name!" Phillip said. "My name is Cowan. Cowan, dammit, but Joseph would never acknowledge that. He would never give me my due. I thought you would, Kirsten. I really thought you would. But you couldn't, could you? You're just like her."

She blinked. *Just like who?* She was never certain

if she spoke the words aloud or just thought them inside her own mind.

"You hate me like she did. God, you even *look* just like her. That's why Joseph had to have you, you know. That's why he started this whole damned scheme. Because of what *she* did to him."

Adam came up the rest of the way, slowly lowering the trapdoor, his eyes on Kirsten's briefly, as if to reassure her.

"She said she loved him, and then she left him," Phillip went on. "And six months later she left me on his doorstep. But he wouldn't claim me as his own. No, not Joe Cowan. He named me Carr, said when I grew up I could be his driver. Big joke. Big effing joke. But I never laughed. He sent me off to be raised by strangers, my beloved father. While my mother went to the next man on her list and married him. But it didn't matter, she left him, too. The second he had his first heart attack. The second she realized he wasn't perfect. No man could ever be good enough for our mother, could he, Kirsten?"

Kirsten's head was buzzing. Adam came closer, using Phillip's distraction to his advantage.

"I wish I'd been the baby she'd kept, instead of you, Kirsten. I really do. I wish she had stayed with Joseph and raised me the way she should have. None of this would have happened if you'd never been born."

The light flashed on in her brain, and it was blinding. For just a moment the shock cut through the drugs and the pain. "My God, are you talking about my mother?"

"Our mother." Phillip smiled sickly. "Sis."

Then he jerked his head and his gun toward Adam. "Stop it! Stop trying to get closer!"

Adam froze, hands high. "Look, we can talk this out. You don't want to do this, Phillip. You don't want to hurt your own sister."

"She hates me! Just like our mother did!" Phillip shrieked. His gun barrel jammed up into the soft underside of her chin now, his hand trembling violently as he backed up the steep, ladderlike stairs, pulling her with him. All that lived at the top was the widow's walk. Three stories up. Sweet heaven.

"Joseph told me all the things you used to say about me, Kirsten. How you called me a bastard. How you swore you'd get everything he had and throw me out without a dime once he was gone. He told me *everything!*"

"He lied to you, Phillip," Kirsten whispered, fighting hard to stay cognizant, to cling to the ability to speak. "He lied. He was a liar, you know that. I didn't even know you were my...I didn't even know."

Phillip shook his head. "At least he let me live here. Gave me a decent job. A home. At least he was my friend. That's more than you ever were."

"He was never anyone's friend, Phillip," Adam said.

"He was the only one I had." Tears streamed down Phillip's cheeks now. "He was my father. You don't have any idea how much it hurt when he made me kill him.''

"Then why did you do it?" Adam asked, his voice accusing. He was getting desperate to stop Phillip. Kirsten could see it in his eyes. The closer they got to the door at the top, the one that opened directly onto the widow's walk, the more distressed Adam looked.

"He *made me*," Phillip moaned. "He had a gun pointed at me, and he put another one in my hand, laid the barrel up against his forehead and kept telling me to do it. Said he'd kill me if I didn't. Called me a weakling and a coward and a fatherless bastard. Said I was so worthless even my own mother hadn't wanted me. Told me the only way I'd ever have anything in my life was if I did what he said, exactly as he said. Pull the trigger, take his gun, leave the other one. He just kept going and going, and then he lifted his own gun to my head and said he'd count to three, and when he got there one of us was going to be on the floor dead. I was crying. I was pleading with him. But he kept counting. When he got to three I...I did it. I shot him. I shot him. I shot him.''

Sobs racked the man. The gun jerked against Kirsten's throat, and it hurt like hell. Phillip shoved the trapdoor open and started up through. She felt a soft breeze, warm sunlight. She blinked in the brightness.

Phillip kicked the door shut after they passed through, and then he stood on top of it, to prevent Adam from coming up. He was still crying.

She could hear Adam scrambling up from inside, hear his frantic efforts to shove the door open. Phillip bounced with the force of Adam's blows from beneath the door.

"I did everything just the way he said I should," Phillip went on. Talking to her, or to himself, or maybe to God. She wasn't sure anymore. "I took the gun he'd been holding…and I wiped all the prints off the one I had shot him with. And then I left it lying there beside him. And I went away. All that was left was to kill you, Kirsten. He said if I did it right, if it looked like an accident or a suicide, I'd get everything. All his money. Everything."

She looked up at him. At the line of his jaw, the crook in his nose. Her brother. Her mother's son. And Joseph's. The enormity of it rocked her. She'd known about her mother's pregnancy by another man. Heard her mother talk about getting rid of the child. And she'd always been aware of her father's hatred for Joseph Cowan. But she'd never put it all together until now.

It shook her to the marrow. But her own impending death shook her even more.

"It's over now, Phillip. Killing me now will do you no good."

"You rejected me," he said. "Just like she did. You never once acknowledged me as your brother, not in all the time you and Joseph lived in that house. You barely even spoke to me."

"I didn't know…."

"I don't have any reason to live now, but I'm damned well not leaving you behind to collect the millions that should have been mine."

''Let us both live,'' she whispered. ''And I'll share it with you.''

He stared down into her eyes, and for a long moment, seemed to be thinking. Then he shook his head. ''They know now. About Joseph. And Hawkins... They'll put me in prison for that. It doesn't matter.'' He glanced down, and she was compelled by some masochistic impulse to do the same. The ground seemed a mile away, and it spun lazily below. He leaned closer to the rail.

''Why did you kill Hawkins?'' she asked in desperation.

Phillip stilled again. ''He drew up the will. And he figured out that I was the one who killed Joseph and guessed I planned to kill you, too.'' He shook his head. ''I wasn't going to at first, you know. I was just going to let you go to prison. You wouldn't have inherited a thing then. I would have gotten it all. But you had to run away. You had to snoop. You and that Adam Brand. And I couldn't risk letting you live, because you might have found out the truth.''

She nodded. ''You didn't want to kill me. Because I'm your sister. Your blood, Phillip. You still don't want to hurt me. I know you don't.''

''I don't have any choice now.'' He blinked at her, his moist brown eyes looking like the eyes of a wounded child. ''You rejected me.''

''Joseph never told me,'' she said again, enunciating each word. ''He never told me, Phillip, I swear!''

''I don't believe you.''

He lunged forward, but taking them to the railing

forced him to remove his weight from the trapdoor. Adam burst up through. Elliot shouted from below, and Kirsten was shocked to see him scaling the steep roof, feet slipping, finding a hold as he risked his life.

But it was too late. Phillip wrenched himself over the rail, clutching her to him as he did. And then he hung there, toes on the very edge, fingers curled around the rail, his back to eternity, one arm anchoring her to his side.

"Don't move. Don't move," he said, to Adam, to her, to Elliot. She was never certain. She only knew neither of the Brands could get to her in time, and she knew Phillip was determined to kill her and himself. If she couldn't get him to let go of her, she was going to die. There was no one to do anything about it but her.

The pen pricked her forearm. She blinked, then worked it into her palm. "Please let me go, Phillip," she whispered.

"I'm sorry. But I can't."

The hand holding the rail let go. At the same time, Kirsten jabbed his other hand—the one holding her captive—with the pen. And it, too, let go.

She scrambled, paddling air with frantic arms, and gripped the rail with one desperate grasp. Phillip fell away behind her. She couldn't look. He never cried out, never made a sound. The thud of his body hitting the earth made her stomach heave. And the weakness caused by the pills he'd force-fed her made her grip tenuous, at best.

"Hold on!" Adam leaned over the rail, clasped her

hand in his. Then he reached for her other hand, the one dangling in space. With firm, quiet power, he hauled her back over the rail and into his arms.

And she thought that in all the time she'd known him, he had never held her as tightly as he did then. Nor had he whispered her name over and over with so much emotion. Nor had he ever, *ever,* dampened her hair with his tears.

Or whispered that he loved her with quite so much conviction.

"I've got you, honey," he kept saying. "God, I'm so sorry. I'm so sorry I walked away. I love you, Kirsten. You hear me? I love you."

Was it the trauma? The stress she'd been under? The pills Phillip had fed her? Was all this some nightmare that had turned itself into her fondest dream? Or could he possibly mean it?

Chapter 14

Adam scooped her up, glanced over the rail and saw Garrett crouched beside Phillip's body. Garrett looked up, met Adam's eyes and shook his head slowly, side to side.

Adam sighed.

"Give me a hand, will you, big brother?" One of Elliot's hands appeared at the railing. Then the other, and then his head rose up behind them.

Cradling Kirsten, Adam reached for his brother with his free hand and helped Elliot over.

"She okay?" Elliot asked, once he got his feet on solid ground.

Adam shifted her weight, examined her face. "I sure as hell hope so. She's been through hell."

"Yeah, and not just today, either."

Elliot opened the trapdoor, then went through first

and watched as Adam followed him down, ready to react if Adam stumbled. His brother seemed to think pretty highly of his woman, Adam thought, not unkindly.

He'd have to ask El to be his best man.

Right after he asked Kirsten to be his wife.

It took forever, he thought, to get down to ground level, but when he did, the whole clan was there waiting. They closed in around Kirsten as he held her. Lash pulled in with the pickup truck, and Wes yanked the door open. "Best get her to a hospital," he said. "She's probably just been fed a half bottle or so of those sleeping pills. She'll be okay, though."

Adam started to ease her into the pickup, but she stirred awake, opened her eyes, looked around at all the concerned faces surrounding her. She sniffed once and bit her lip. "You all...you all came here to help me?"

"'Course we did," Penny said. "And it's all over now. You're gonna be fine."

"But...but..." She stiffened a little in Adam's arms as she looked up at him. "Do they know...do they know what I did?"

"We know," Jessi said, and she reached out to stroke Kirsten's hair. "And it doesn't matter, Kirsten."

"It was an accident," Garrett added.

"And besides, you were just a kid," Wes said.

"Honey, we all make mistakes," Ben told her. And offered her a smile of encouragement.

"Besides," Elliot declared, "you're family."

She shook her head slowly, eyes wide with disbelief. "I don't know what to say."

"Say you'll come to us next time you get in trouble, Kirsten," Penny told her. "We'll be there for you if you ever do. Promise."

Adam lifted Kirsten and settled her into the pickup truck. Then he went around to the other side and got in. As he put the vehicle into motion, Kirsten leaned against him, and he slipped his arm around her shoulders.

"Is Phillip...?" she whispered.

Adam swallowed hard. "He didn't make it. I'm sorry, Kirsty."

He felt the shudder that went through her. "He...he was my brother."

"I know. I know, hon." He held her closer, and she cried softly for a long time.

When her tears eased, she lifted her head. Her eyes were clouded, dim, but she seemed more coherent than before. "I want to see my father," she told him. "I...I need to explain...everything."

"We'll do that when we go to pick him up, Kirsten. The second Doc gives you a clean bill of health and Garrett clears things up with the rangers, we're heading for Dallas. All right?"

She blinked up at him. "We...we are?"

Adam nodded. "I know your head's swimming right now, hon, but I've got some things to say to you that are gonna bust a hole in my gut if I don't get them out."

"All...all right."

"I was a fool, Kirsten. I was a fool two years ago for not loving you enough. For letting you walk away from me. For not believing in what we had enough to know you wouldn't have done that of your own free will. I should have come after you, Kirsten, but I ran away instead, and I'm sorry for that."

He glanced down at her, checking to make sure she was still awake and alert. She needed to hear him, to understand him. He figured he probably ought to wait until Doc had cleared her system of whatever was floating around in it to tell her all of this, but dammit, he *couldn't* wait.

"I'm even sorrier I walked away this time. When you told me the truth. But it was grief, Kirsten. It was shock, and anger, and it didn't mean a damn thing. Shoot, I wasn't gone twenty minutes before I knew I was making a big mistake. And it turned out to be twenty minutes that damn near cost your life. Can you forgive me, Kirsten?"

She drew a deep breath, seemed to be struggling to keep him in focus, blinking and squinting by turns. "There's nothing to forgive, Adam. I'm the one who needs forgiveness, if you can give it. And I'll understand if you can't."

"You're wrong about that," he told her. "I understand—hell, the whole family understands now—what you went through, how it all ended up at this point. No one blames you."

"*I* blame me."

"Well, you shouldn't. Because I don't. Kirsten, I'm back, one hundred percent. And I'm not going to walk away from you again. Now I know I told you that before, but I mean it this time. I'll swear it on my daddy's grave, if it'll help you believe in me again—''

"I never stopped believing in you, Adam."

He glanced down at her as he pulled in to Doc's driveway. "Then give me another chance, Kirsty. Let's start over. Let's have that wedding we planned and buy that ranch we wanted. Let's bring your father home to live with us. I want all those things Cowan stole from us. And I think you do, too. We can have them, Kirsty. All of them. All we have to do is reach out and take them."

Tears brimmed in her eyes. Adam reached up to brush them away. "Say you'll marry me, honey."

"You...you really want to marry me? Even after all I've done...?"

"I've never wanted anything else," he told her. "Not really. I convinced myself I did, for a while, but that was bull. I love you, Kirsten. I need you. This whole family needs you."

Her tears were streaming now.

"So will you marry me, Kirsten? Will you be my wife the way you should have been all along?"

"You know I will," she whispered. "I will."

Adam leaned down and pressed his mouth to hers. She kissed him back for a moment, and then went limp in his arms. He could taste the salt of tears on his lips. But when he lifted his head away, she was out cold. "Lord help me," he said. "I sure as hell hope you meant that."

Then he scooped her up and carried her into Doc's office.

Epilogue

Kirsten stood in front of a three-way mirror. She hadn't been able to shut the tears off long enough yet to apply any makeup, and she was thinking she might have to do without it for the ceremony, because the past few days had been one surprise after another.

Besides, she didn't need it as much anymore. She didn't have to hide now. Adam knew all her secrets...and he loved her anyway.

He loved her anyway.

When she and Adam had picked her father up in Dallas to bring him home once and for all, her father had told her his own secrets. He'd known all along that her first wedding to Adam had never taken place. That something had gone wrong. He'd just been biding his time in the nursing home, hoping to get his strength back enough to come back to Quinn and find out what had happened to throw his little girl's life so far offtrack.

He'd held her while she'd cried. And then the second surprise came. He'd handed her a huge box, gaily wrapped. And she'd opened it up to find the wedding gown—the one she'd left behind, along with all her dreams, over two years ago.

"You saved it?" she'd whispered. "But...but how...when?"

"It doesn't matter," he'd said, and hugged her. "I always knew the day would come when you'd need it again. Now, go and put it on. I never got to see you in it the first time you wore it, and I think I've waited long enough."

So had she. The dress still fit, and it felt right. Perfect. Even more now than it had before.

There was a tap on the door to the tiny room at the back of the chapel. "Can I come in yet?" her father asked through the wood.

"Yes, Daddy. Come in."

He opened the door, and she turned in a rustle of ivory satin. "My, my," he whispered. "I've never seen anything so beautiful in all my days." Her father's blue eyes teared up as he held out his arms, and she rushed into them.

"I'm going to make up for everything, Daddy," she whispered. "You're going to be so happy with Adam and me."

"So long as you're happy, sweetheart, I will be, too."

"We all will be," she promised.

A throat cleared, and she drew back from her father's embrace to look toward the doorway. Elliot stood there, holding a bouquet and looking drop-dead gorgeous in his tux. "Can I come in? I could come back later...."

"Come in," Kirsten said.

He did, tugging at his collar. He handed her the bouquet of lilies and orchids, with their draping ivory ribbons. "Adam wanted me to bring this to you...and, uh, to make sure you had everything you needed."

She lifted her brows. "And to make sure I didn't forget to show up this time?"

Elliot smiled. "I didn't say that."

"No, but I'll bet he did."

"He knows you'll be there, hon. But you know, as best man, I figured I'd double-check. There is a back way out of here, after all. I could just picture my brother if you should get abducted by aliens or something, and be late. He'd probably pass out cold." Elliot was grinning, that infectious, happy smile of his that never failed to ooze charm. "I've never seen him so nervous."

A whole chorus of female voices rose from the hallway, and Kirsten turned in time to see her beautiful sisters-in-law piling into the room. Chelsea was straightening a stray bit of Taylor's hair, while Taylor smoothed a fold in the hem of Jessi's dress and Jessi picked a piece of lint from Chelsea's shoulder. They all stopped fussing when they looked at Kirsten. They went still, then started talking all at once.

Then they shooed the men out and descended on

her in one mass, wielding combs, brushes, makeup and jewelry.

It wasn't long before she was ready. The organ music swelled from the small chapel, and Kirsten licked her lips. "Oh, gosh," she whispered. "Okay, here goes."

Chelsea stood in the doorway and helped little Maria Michele—who'd been walking for only a month now—and Bubba get started. Bubba held the toddler's hand, obviously feeling like a big strong Brand man already, assisting his little cousin down the aisle.

Chelsea followed. Then Taylor, and then Jessi.

Penny, as maid of honor, went next. Kirsten peered through a crack in the door of the little room at the back of the church and watched her progress. Her father squeezed her hand when her turn came. She squeezed back.

He took her arm, and they started down the aisle. She looked up, saw Adam standing there at the other end, waiting for her, and knew that her life was finally beginning. His eyes met hers. He mouthed, "I love you."

"I love you, too," she whispered back. "I love you, too."

* * * * *

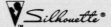

If you enjoyed what you just read,
then we've got an offer you can't resist!

Take 2 bestselling love stories FREE!

Plus get a FREE surprise gift!

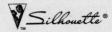

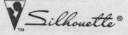

INTIMATE MOMENTS®
Silhouette®

COMING NEXT MONTH

#913 ROYAL'S CHILD—Sharon Sala
The Justice Way

Royal Justice knew he would do anything to make his daughter happy. So when she insisted that a lone hitchhiker needed *their* help, he went against his better judgment and told Angel Rojas to climb on board. After that, it didn't take long before his two favorite females were giving him a few lessons on how to live—and love—again.

#914 CULLEN'S BRIDE—Fiona Brand
March Madness

Sexy Cullen Logan thought he had no chance for a happy family—until he met Rachel Sinclair. She was everything he'd ever wanted in a woman, and now she was about to have his child. Cullen knew that being a father was a full-time job, but given his dangerous past, was he qualified for the position?

#915 A TRUE-BLUE TEXAS TWOSOME—Kim McKade
March Madness

Toby Haskell was perfectly content with his life as a country sheriff. Until his one true love, Corrine Maxwell, returned to town. Losing her had been hard—and accepting it even harder. Now she was back, and he knew he had a second chance. But was his small-town life enough for a big-city girl?

#916 THE MAN BEHIND THE BADGE—Vickie Taylor
March Madness

The last thing FBI agent Jason Stateler needed was to get too close to his sexy female partner. But Lane McCullough was part of the case, and he knew he wasn't going away—and, secretly, he didn't really want her to. Tracking down a criminal was easy—it was their unexpected passion that was going to be the problem.

#917 DANGEROUS CURVES—Kristina Wright
March Madness

Samantha Martin knew she was innocent of murder—she'd just been in the wrong place at the wrong time. And so was Jake Cavanaugh, because he had been foolish enough to pick her up when she was making her escape. But now there was no turning back, and before long she was trusting him with her life...but what about with her heart?

#918 THE MOTHER OF HIS CHILD—Laurey Bright
Conveniently Wed

The moment Charisse Lane most feared had arrived: her child's father had found them! More disconcerting was her immediate, intense attraction to the tall, dark dad—an attraction Daniel Richmond clearly reciprocated. But Charisse knew that a legacy of lies—and secrets—could very well prevent the happily-ever-after she wished could be theirs....